Across the Great Divide

Book 2 - The Search

By Michael L. Ross

Cover designed by Jenny Quinlan:
HistoricalFictionBookCovers.com

Michael L. Ross

Visit my website at
http://www.HistoricalNovelsRUs.com
Facebook: historicalnovelsrus
Twitter: @MichaellRoss7

Printed in the United States of America
First Printing: December 2020
HistoricalNovelsRUs
ISBN 978-1-7359931-0-2

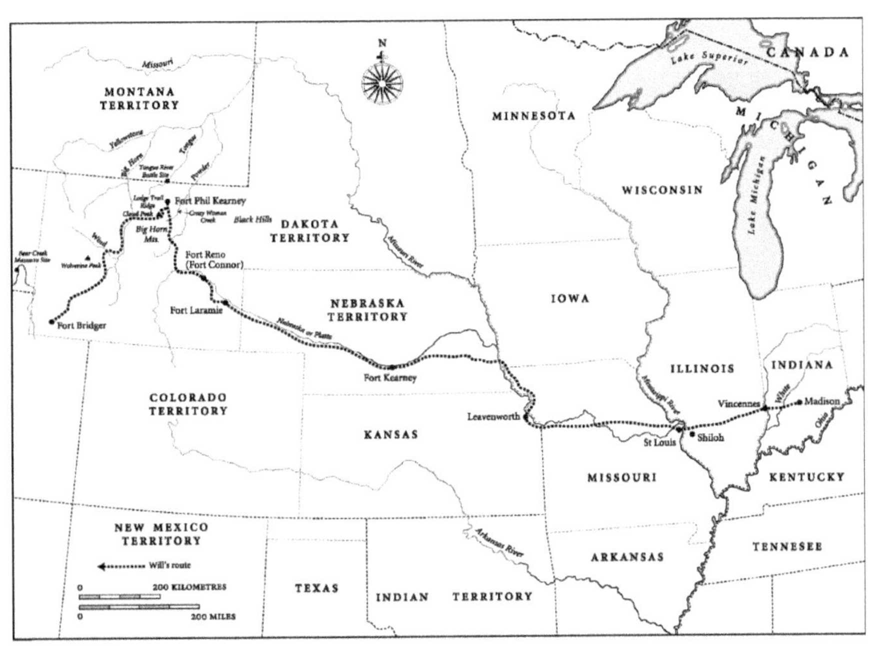

Will's Journey

Dedicated to the thousands of Native Americans that perished at the hands of the US Army and disease.

Contents

CHAPTER ONE

June 1865, Indiana

Voices in Will's head accused him of murder, cowardice, and betrayal. Peace eluded him. Memories of the war and prison crowded in, mocking him. When he stopped at night, sleep was absent. Except for God, he was alone—and even God felt distant.

After leaving his sister's farm in Madison, he made camp in a clearing outside the village of Washington, Indiana. Lightning, dark clouds and wind threatened from the southwest. A grove of hemlock and black ash made a natural circle, promising protection. There were no beautiful orange and pink tones—the sky looked black, clouds hugging the hills and roiling in circles, mirroring the storm in his soul. The wind was bending the trees and blowing the scent of rain.

Will set up camp and got a small fire going. Best to cook supper before it became impossible. He brought water from a nearby creek and soon had a pot of beans boiling, mixing with the smell of coffee. He added garlic and onions to the beans. Albinia had insisted he take the seasonings with him. Within half an hour, the dark clouds produced drops of rain sizzling into the fire. Will wolfed his supper and rinsed the tin plate. He checked Dusty's tether and hobble one more time, in case he spooked. The horse snorted, his eyes dilated at the escalating sound of thunder.

Will retreated to his bedroll and tent, sitting and looking out at the rain. Maybe he was foolish—here he was in the middle of a plains thunderstorm when he could be in the snug cabin at Albinia's, with family around. But that was the problem—family. He needed to be alone. For the safety of his family, he couldn't stay with them. Just before he left, his little sister Lydia had awakened him, and he'd almost shot her before he knew what he was doing, thinking himself back in the war.

His nerves were stretched taut. Being in Indiana brought back the war and Morgan's raid. He'd made peace with his father, but . . . Will hated to admit that being around him triggered his memories. His mind saw his black horse leaping the barricade in Madison, a blue-clad soldier swinging a rifle, knocking him out of the saddle. He'd rolled, aiming a pistol—to find it pointed at his father. The experience had shaken him. He relived it in his mind, over and over. The former slave, Luther, the battle at Ashland—there were just too many memories that trailed behind him, like the ball and chain he'd worn at Camp Douglas for a time.

He loved his family too much to risk hurting them and losing them forever. If he could figure out what was wrong with him—if he could bury the ghosts that came to haunt him, maybe then there could be peace, home, and family.

He stared into the fading embers of the fire as the skies opened in earnest. A flash of sheet lightning lit up the sky, casting eerie shadows. Face after face came to his mind; the thunder cracks became cannon blasts. He remembered the storm after the first day of Shiloh. And all his friends during the war—Tom Morgan, Archie, Peter—so many who died depending on him to protect them. The face of the first Federal he'd shot, protecting John Morgan. One by one, they marched up in his mind, forming a jury, condemning him forever. And Jenny—where had he been when she'd needed protection? Off fighting for Morgan. He hadn't defended his home at all—the very people he protected had burned it to the ground. Thunder roared again, and he realized he was sweating and shaking.

Another lightning flash—what was that movement across the clearing? There were eyes, green eyes like burning coals. They were moving toward him. Were the ghosts of his dreams coming for revenge? Jagged forks of lightning lit the sky, and he saw a canine form. Could it be a wolf? A coyote looking for the remains of his supper? What would be prowling in this storm instead of curled up in a den?

The eyes came closer. Will checked the load on his Navy Colt and leveled it at the intruder. There was no growl or aggressive action. The animal crept closer. The fire was down to sparks, but the shape traveled around it in a wide berth. Another brief flash revealed a brindle dog a few feet away. The face was like a bulldog, the body large, two feet tall at the shoulder. Instead of growling, the dog lay down and whimpered. Will holstered the Colt, deciding the animal posed no threat. He rummaged in the saddlebag beside him and held out a piece of jerky.

When the dog didn't move closer, he whispered, "Here, boy. No one's going to hurt you. Take it." The animal crept forward a few inches but stopped. Will tossed the meat to within a few inches of his nose. He sniffed it, then devoured it in a single bite. Will held out his hand, palm down, fingers drooped, to indicate friendship. After a minute, the dog rewarded him by rising, walking closer, and sniffing Will's fingers, no doubt looking for more of the meat. Their meager supplies would be exhausted if he kept feeding him. He patted the dog's head, getting his fingers licked in return. Will patted the space in the tent beside him, and the dog padded into the tent, lying next to him. He'd made a new friend.

Will awoke to the sound of a lonesome train whistle in the distance. The dog was lapping his face. Pushing the mutt away hard, he jumped to his feet, shook his head, and stretched. The storm had blown through, the sun was bright, and the sky azure blue. How had he slept so long?

Will wondered about the dog—was he a stray from some nearby farm? In the morning light, he appeared shaggy, bedraggled, and skinny, with powerful shoulders. Either his owner didn't take good care of him, or the dog had no owner. Will's stomach rumbled as he pulled out a piece of the jerky and hardtack. The dog looked at him with longing eyes. He sighed and found another piece of jerky. If the dog stayed, he would have to hunt soon.

A gray rabbit hopped into view, lolling in the prairie grass, sitting up and gazing around for danger. Will drew the Colt, taking deliberate aim. No time to get the rifle from the saddle sheath. His finger inched the trigger back. The pistol roared, the world blurred, and he was back on the battlefield, minié balls whining around him and bayonets flashing. The smell of powder, the cries of the wounded, the sound of exploding shells—it all came back in an instant. Will's hand shook. His forehead dripped sweat as the prairie came back into focus. The shot had gone wide. Breathing hard, he dropped the pistol. It was the first time he'd fired a gun since the war. He hadn't been expecting that reaction. What would he do if he hallucinated every time he shot a gun?

He sat down, resting and getting his bearings. After his breathing slowed, he packed and saddled Dusty. The horse had weathered the night fine. Will rode a short distance and turned to see whether the dog followed. He did. He decided to name the dog. He had the look of a bull mastiff and seemed to lope along, having no trouble keeping up with Dusty. Rustler? Naw, he was nothing like the dog of his childhood. Lightning? Since he'd come out of the storm? Yeah! That seemed like a good name. It would take a little time to teach it to him—if he stuck around long enough to learn. He pulled an oilskin from his saddlebag, opened it, and took out a map, making plans and charting a route.

The sun angled higher in the sky, and he pushed Dusty into a slow trot. He came to the banks of the White River and, finding a low spot, started across. Would Lightning balk at the water? If so, he'd have to leave him—where he was going was no place for a dog afraid of rivers. The river came to just below his stirrups, and Dusty forded it, clambering up on the opposite bank. Looking back, he saw Lightning swimming well, undisturbed by the current. He joined them on the bank and looked up at Will as if to ask, "What next?"

"You know, Lightning, you could be helpful. But I can't afford to feed you from my supplies."

The dog never slackened his pace or indicated that he heard, though soon he was streaking off across the grassland, chasing something. A few minutes later, he reappeared, trotting toward Will with a prairie chicken dangling from his jaws.

"Whatcha got there? Hmm, looks like lunch for both of us."

They halted for a few hours to pluck and roast the chicken. True to his word, Will gave Lightning half, as well as many words of praise.

As dusk fell, Will saw firelight and a wagon to the right of the trail. A cheerful fiddle tune and the smell of roasting meat wafted across the prairie. Will wondered if it might be a family that would let him bunk with them for the night. The fiddle music stopped.

The man of the family stood, rifle in hand, cocked and waiting. "Evening."

"Evening. Y'all mind if I bunk near your wagon tonight?"

"Where you headed?"

"Out beyond Leavenworth. You?"

"On to Oregon. We hear there's good land there. Where you from?"

"Kentucky. I got some jerky. Not looking to impose for food, just a little company and a safer bed for the night."

The man looked him over in the growing twilight. His brow furrowed, then relaxed as he made a decision, lowering the rifle.

"All right. You can bunk under the wagon—you look honest enough. Just remember, if anything's missing in the morning, I can shoot the eye out of a bird at two hundred yards."

Will touched his hat and climbed down. Lightning came up beside him. "This stray adopted me about twenty miles back. He'll take care of himself and won't be any trouble."

The man looked at the size of the dog. "I got kids here. He hurts one of them, he's dead."

"Fair enough. As I said, the dog won't be trouble."

The rifle motioned toward the fire, and Will tethered Dusty to the wagon on a ring, grabbing some grub from his saddlebag.

He moved over to take a seat on a log. He had focused on the man and now saw a woman in a gingham bonnet and two children crowded close to her, looking shy and afraid.

The woman was silent. Standing, she offered him a cup of coffee.

"Thanks, ma'am. I hope I'm no trouble for you. Have you seen many people on the trail?"

"There's been a few wagons. It's late in the year, but we heard tell of another wagon train about to head west out of Independence. We're hoping to catch it and join up. Might winter at one of the forts along the way."

"Hope you find what you're after. Know of any good crossings ahead? I hear the Wabash is deep."

The man turned and said, "Vincennes, town due west about twenty miles. They have a good bridge. The story goes that Lincoln crossed it, going from Kentuck to Illinois."

"Much obliged—guess I'll make for that, then."

Will got up and going early the next day, leaving without waking the family.

Fear settled on Will like an unwelcome blanket in the summer heat. The thought of entering Fort Leavenworth and being among Union soldiers made him sweat. It brought back the prison guards, the war, and the memories he was fleeing. After crossing the river into Kansas, the real journey west would begin, but he wouldn't think of that yet. He just wanted to find a real bed for the night, a meal cooked by someone else, and good oats for Dusty. Tomorrow he would think about the journey beyond civilization, out on the Oregon Trail. He wasn't planning on going all the way to Oregon—just to the mountains, to lose himself in their quiet solitude. Will wanted to escape the reminders of the war, to find peace.

Today the demon that stalked him was the memory of how he had failed his men at Buffington Island. Years of prison, starving, freezing, and many friends dying of smallpox and exposure. He shook his head and forced his concentration on the blue sky.

The brick-and-stone buildings of the town and the fort seemed out of place on the vast prairie, as though somehow they had been dropped like the toy blocks of a giant, discarded play things that would be left to ruin. He needed supplies and information, or he would have avoided the fort altogether. Will hadn't been sleeping well—the dreams were back. He felt exhausted and drained. His body hadn't recovered from being a prisoner of war at Camp Douglas. Riding tired him more than he would have thought after all the miles he'd traveled during the war.

All the prison memories—crowded together, freezing, starving, holding the hands of the dying. So many lost to the ravages of war and disease . . . How could he ever forget and pretend life was normal?

He stopped about a half-mile from the ferry, dismounted, and tied Dusty to a tree. Lightning sat by Dusty, tail thumping the ground, looking at Will and whining. Before he got to the fort, he'd better find out if shooting would trigger a hallucination. What if the soldiers fired a salute at the fort? If he was going to shake, better to do it here, alone, than later in front of Federals. He paced out twenty yards and set up a target. It should be child's play; he'd hit targets at that distance almost from the time he could shoot. Walking back to Dusty, he spun, aimed, and fired, not giving himself time to think. His hand faltered at the last moment, somehow anticipating the shot, and it went wild by several feet. His heart pounded, his breathing quickened, but no visions came—an improvement. He had to get over this. Once he left Leavenworth, he'd be depending on his gun for food and defense.

An idea occurred to him: What if he couldn't hear the gunshot? He wouldn't know whether he'd fired until the gun kicked and the shot was away. He tried stuffing bits of cloth from his saddlebag in his ears. He emptied the revolver of all but one cartridge so he wouldn't know whether it would fire each time. He tried again, over and over, until he could master his breathing and not flinch.

Walking back to Dusty, he mounted and saw the ferry just coming back from the other side of the river. A glance at the sun told him not to wait much longer, lest the ferryman shut down for the night. They trotted down to the ferry, paid their fare, and boarded. The ferryman glared at Lightning but gave no argument when the dog hopped aboard.

Once across the river, Will looked for a place to camp. The dusk grew, and he wasn't sure he could handle blue uniforms on top of his episode after shooting. The fort and a bed would have to wait.

The sun was well above the horizon when Will packed up his tent and bedroll. He pointed Dusty at a walk toward the fort. Seeing the Federal sentry, he shivered even with the warm sun at his back. He wanted to turn away, to escape.

The guard gave him a bored glance, waving him through. Will asked directions to the sutler's and rode there, tying Dusty to a rail. He concentrated his gaze on the ground in front of him, on his immediate surroundings, trying to ignore the swarm of blue uniforms scurrying ant-like around the buildings of the fort. The sutler was just off the parade ground, near the enlisted quarters. Lightning looked up at Will and whined.

"No, I doubt they want you inside. Sit. You'll have to wait with Dusty."

Lightning lay down, head between his paws.

Will went inside and waited for his turn at the counter.

"Yes, Sir? How may I help you?"

"I need two weeks' supply of jerky and hardtack, a hundred cartridges for my Spencer, two pounds of powder, a hundred percussion caps, and two pounds of lead."

"Planning on starting a war, or just a bad shot?" joked the sutler.

"Neither," Will said. "Long trip ahead."

"You may find cartridges for the Spencer scarce out west. I have a few hundred myself, but they're reserved for the Army. 'Course, the arsenal has more, but . . . Sure I couldn't interest you in a Sharps?"

"How much? I used a Whitworth in the war."

"Army likes the Spencers, but the paper cartridges for the Sharps are easier to make or find. Tell you what, I'll take your Spencer on trade and let you have the Sharps for fifteen dollars."

"How much for the Sharps without the trade?"

"Forty."

"Thirty-five and a Bowie knife."

"Done."

Will counted out the gold pieces and laid the knife on the counter.

"Any place around here a fellow can practice shooting without raising a ruckus?"

"Don't see why not. Go northwest of the fort, inland from the river. Don't go south—Delaware Indian reservation."

"Much obliged," said Will, picking up his order. "And where can I get a bed? Is there a hotel around here, or do people stay at the fort?"

The sutler scratched his balding head. "Well, the barracks prob'ly has some empty beds right now. Begging your pardon, by your accent I'm guessing you're Southern. The commander might not be favorable to you staying here. But you could ask."

"Much obliged."

"There's a performance of Hamlet at the theater after the funeral, if you're bored. We try to have a little culture in the wilderness."

"Funeral?"

"Couple soldiers died. Some say it was cholera, though the commander don't want that whispered too loud."

"I'll just find a bed and some grub. How much extra for some jerky for my dog?"

"Ten cents."

"Kinda high, but I won't argue."

Tipping his hat and gathering his supplies, he packed everything on Dusty. The two rifles went into scabbards on each side. He decided he would concentrate his shooting practice on the Colt and the Sharps since he could make lead balls, and ammunition for the Spencer was more precious.

Once he'd loaded his supplies on Dusty, he sat on a bench outside the store, reloading the Colt and petting Lightning without thinking. Will put in the standard five balls, leaving one chamber empty for safety.

Looking over near the water trough, he saw a leather-skinned Indian, face wrinkled with age, staring at him. He looked away, rubbing his neck. Should he find out why the old man was staring? He wasn't sure they could communicate. Maybe the Indian just wanted some food. He holstered the pistol and rummaged in his saddlebag for some of the jerky, holding it out to the old man.

The Indian came over and took it.

"Do you speak English?" asked Will.

"Yes. Mission school. But most Indians won't. Are you new on the prairie?"

"Yes."

"The tribes don't all speak the same tongue. There is a way, though. Signs. There is a set of signs that anyone can understand."

"Can you teach me?"

The old man considered. "Perhaps. If you give some coffee and jerky, I will teach."

For the next few hours, Will watched, concentrating on learning to turn words into motions.

His teacher rubbed arthritic hands together and rose. "Enough.

I am old and tired. Come again tomorrow—if you have more to trade."

Will watched the old man leave and saw a funeral party forming, soldiers loading a flag-draped coffin onto a flatbed wagon. The honor detail formed up. A bugler blew "Taps." The honor detail prepared to fire the salute.

At the roar of the cannon and the sound of rifles, Will jumped from his seat and drew his pistol. He smelled the smoke from the cannon, heard the cries of the wounded. Dirt spewed up around him as shells hit. Tree branches split with canister shot. The whine of minié balls sounded like a swarm of angry wasps. Horses neighed in terror. Confederates and Federals drew up in battle lines along the trees of the Shiloh field. A gray form beside him fell, clutching his chest, a fountain of blood spurting. Will ducked behind a fallen log. Another friend fell, his skull opened by a Federal cartridge. Brains splattered across his shirt. Was his gun loaded? He didn't remember. Federals were running toward him, bayonets extended. Fumbling with the gun, he checked his load. He dropped and rolled, then ran toward the Federal lines. His commander, Duke, was urging him to follow, sword upraised. Will ran, then kneeled, and, aiming at the nearest Federal, his gun went off just as something hit him hard from behind.

Will woke, pain pounding from the lump on his head. He rose to a sitting position. There were bars on the window, and it looked as though the door to the little room was locked. He must be in the stockade. He tried not to panic and took a deep breath. How did he get here? What happened to Dusty? And Lightning? Had the Federals stolen everything and thrown him in jail?

He attempted to stand but fell back. He realized he was thirsty. How long had he been here? He reached for his holster and gun, but they were gone. Panic rose. An unbidden scream escaped his throat as he began beating on the walls. No one heard; no one came.

Will tried again, this time staggering over to the window.

"Guard! Guard!" he called.

A corporal with a bar-handled mustache came over.

"What's the problem?"

"I'm in here, that's the problem! Where are my things? Where's my horse and my dog? Why am I here?"

"Well, when you disrupt a major's funeral and shoot at someone, what do you expect? You're in there until the commander can decide what to do with you. Now you're up and around, he'll maybe see you tomorrow."

Will beat on the walls. "I want out! Now! I haven't done anything—I don't remember anything!"

The corporal ignored him. "Private Yates! Fetch this man a water pail and a chamber pot."

Turning back to Will, he said, "I'm bringing you water and food if you settle down. Private Yates will be outside the door with a rifle aimed at your head, in case you get ideas when the door opens. I suggest you lie down and be quiet. The doc will come and look at you before dark."

"Can you at least find my dog and let him in with me?"

"He's tied up over at the stable. Doubt they'd let him in here. Near took a hand off the soldiers that picked you up."

Will spent a restless night on the hard bunk. Flies and mosquitoes buzzed with high, whining frequency around his head. He couldn't lie on his back as he was used to since that made his head wound push against the logs of the bunk. He was a little afraid to sleep anyway— what would they do if they heard him screaming in a dream? After hours sitting in the dark, he couldn't keep his eyes open.

He woke just before dawn, when there was gray light in the sky. He shivered with cold, though the morning promised a hot day. He'd dreamed of standing out in the frigid air at Camp Douglas, with the commander screaming at him to confess. He had a new bruise on his arm from banging against the logs of the wall in his dreams.

He saw they'd brought his pack. Wonder if they'd ransacked it? Checking under his shirt, Will felt the comforting bulge of the money pouch—they hadn't robbed him of that, at least. He looked in the pack, found his Bible, and tried to read. His head throbbed. Will gave it up, praying instead. He found himself angry with God for all the suffering and pain he'd witnessed and endured. "Lord, why bring me all this way to rot in jail again? What about your ever-present help in times of trouble? WHY?"

After about an hour, the private came with a tin plate of rations.

"Eat quick, Reb. Colonel Grierson wants to see you right away."

Will finished and banged the plate on the wall.

The private returned. "You gonna come peaceful, or do I need to put you in irons?"

"No need for that. I won't make trouble."

They walked across the parade ground to the colonel's quarters.

Will fiddled with his hat, showing his nerves. Grierson entered.

"Have a seat, son. I hear you've been shooting up my fort."

"No, Sir. I mean, I don't remember, Sir. I heard a cannon and woke up in jail. I don't know what happened in between."

"You don't remember firing a revolver at the funeral detail? Or putting a hole in the rain barrel and a soldier's cap?"

"No, Sir. I . . . I've been having episodes, Sir. Where it feels like I'm back in the war or back in Camp Douglas. Please, Sir, I meant no harm."

"I'm not sure Corporal Robinson would agree with you,

judging from the hole in his hat."

"Sir, I fought at Shiloh. I was a sharpshooter. Now I'm trying not to jump at the sound of a cannon. Or blue uniforms, begging your pardon. It would be safest for all concerned if I got out of the fort and went on my way. I don't believe the fighting and the Confederacy were right anymore, but I'd given my word to General Morgan, and I kept it. With due respect, the war is over, and I don't wish anyone harm. I want to go far away, rest, and find peace."

"Maybe turning you loose on the Arapaho and Cheyenne is a good idea. It would save me a lot of paperwork. It's quiet right now on the plains—they've traveled north, or so my scouts tell me. If the scouts are wrong, I'd be signing your death warrant, letting you go out there. You should wait for a wagon train, go with a group."

"Are you saying you're letting me go?"

"Maybe I shouldn't, but yes. I've seen enough killing in the war, and I know other men affected like you. I hope you find your peace, son. You're free to go. See the quartermaster to draw your belongings. Be off the post within an hour, and don't come back soon."

Will stood and saluted. "Yes, Sir! Thank you, Sir!"

"Watch out for your hair, young man. It's a rough world west of here."

"Best directions to the Emigrant Trail, sir?"

"Head northwest toward Fort Kearney. You'll run into it. So many pilgrims going over it, you won't miss it."

Will collected his belongings. Lightning seemed none the worse for the experience, though he growled at the stable boy when Will came to get him. By noon, Will was miles from the fort. He stopped by a creek, in the scarce shade of a tree. After nooning on hardtack and water, he again took the time to set up targets and practiced. Shooting needed to become second nature again. At least here, if he had a hallucination, no one was around to see it. After the colonel's description of the trail, it would be important not to have the problem around a wagon train.

Again, he tried the pistol, remembering this time to use his ear protection. Instead of trying rapid-fire, he took careful aim and paid attention to his breathing. The small rocks he was using for targets danced in the dust sprayed by the shots. Better, he thought. He heard a slight muffled sound from the gun. Owing to the uncertainty of ammunition, he decided against trying the Spencer and pulled out the Sharps. He built a fire, found his bullet mold, and made ten cartridges. He scanned the prairie and saw a boulder jutting up about four hundred yards distant.

Will knelt and sighted the unfamiliar gun. He counted to five, squeezed the trigger, let out some of his breath, paused, and squeezed some more. The rifle bucked, and the shot hit low. He reloaded, adjusted, and tried again. Dust flew from the target. He looked over to see how Lightning was taking the gunfire, but the dog seemed unfazed. He repeated the procedure, but this time when he sighted and started to squeeze, he didn't see the stone—he saw a Federal soldier, inching forward on the ground where the rock should have been. Will dropped his gaze, counted to ten, looked up, and didn't see the soldier. He looked around himself, praying, thanking God for every leaf and branch, then shut his eyes for a full minute. When he opened them, he spent a few minutes more petting Lightning and giving him jerky. The dog made him feel more connected to the present.

Will tried the shot several times, each time focusing on what was around him. He knew this would detract from his aim, but better a little off than catapulted back to the war. Determined, he kept trying. He was going to beat this.

He mounted and rode out to his target rock, putting the rifle in its sheath. He could see groupings that grew closer to the center of the stone. His accuracy was making progress.

After riding a few hours, he made camp and fell into a night of blessed, dreamless sleep.

With the dawn, Will woke up with a stiff back and decided to stretch and limber up. He pondered how to make jerky and hardtack taste different and gave up, just warming the jerky over the fire, throwing some to Lightning. A prairie chicken flew up a short distance away, and without thinking, he drew his pistol and fired. The bird dropped, and he followed its descent, focusing on every detail. Lightning raced after it, bringing it back. Putting himself in the moment and in touch with God was working to combat the hallucinations. Maybe he wasn't going crazy after all.

CHAPTER TWO

A high scream of terror echoed from the buttes, coming from over the hill ahead. Will's heart jumped. He drew his Spencer rifle from the saddle scabbard. Two months traveling had taught him caution. Rather than charge forward, he urged his quarter horse off the trail, circling to the left. The screaming continued, then faded to a repetitive chant. Will didn't understand the words, but they had a rhythm, and the note of fear in the voice was unmistakable. The singing stopped, and silence descended. As he came to the top of the rise, he dismounted, cocking the Spencer rifle and levering a round into the chamber. He tied the horse to a scrub tree and told Lightning to stay. The dog barked and growled, hair standing up on its neck.

Peering over a boulder, he saw a huge brown bear twenty yards away, up on hind legs. It towered eight feet above the prairie, silvered brown fur and long claws flashing in the sun. The bear huffed several times, sniffing the air, head weaving back and forth. An Indian woman cowered under a scrub pine, clutching a long knife. The bear crashed down on all four feet. She backed away, putting the trunk of the tree between them. On the ground lay a sizeable six-point buck. The deer ribs showed claw marks. Blood flowed from the neck. Had the woman surprised the bear with its kill? She waited for the bear's next move. The massive beast continued to paw at the ground, a few feet separating bear and woman, the deer lying between them.

The woman was chanting again in a low voice, clutching the large knife. The grizzly sniffed the air and looked in Will's direction. Lightning whined and scratched the ground. What if the dog charged the bear? Should he shoot? The sharpshooter in him wanted to act. Or would that enrage the bear and endanger the woman? What if he hallucinated after the shot? He stuffed rags in his ears to dull the sound of the gun. The bear reached a huge paw out, huffed twice, and rolled the deer over. After taking a bite, it shook its head, lifting the whole carcass from the ground. Then it dropped the meat, galloped around the tree, mouth open, showing giant teeth. It leaped at the woman. She dodged again, striking at one of the enormous paws with her knife. The bear sank its teeth into her arm, making her drop the blade. When it opened its jaws, she rolled onto her stomach and curled into a tight ball to protect as much of her body as possible, waiting for the inevitable. The bear grunted and reached to roll her over.

Will leveled the rifle at the bear. After firing two fifty-six caliber rounds in quick succession just above the bear's shoulder, he aimed a third at its head.

The world swam in front of Will's eyes. The sound of the rifle became the sound of a battlefield. He saw his friends dying, blue uniforms advancing, smelled the smoke from cannons—his heart pounded, and he felt crippling fear. He was frozen, knowing that he could not save his friends. Then the battle faded, and the prairie came back into focus.

After getting his bearings, Will rose and crept toward the rear of the tree, not knowing what he would find. When he was close enough, he could see the bear lying still on its side. He was sure he'd hit the bear, but he couldn't be sure it was dead. The woman wasn't moving. Was she still alive?

As he inched closer, he saw her chest rise, taking a breath. Blood dripped from the gash on her arm. Maybe she'd fainted? The bear still wasn't moving and appeared dead. He laid the rifle down, took the rags out of his ears, and walked toward her with one hand cupped over the other at his chest. If she woke up, maybe she would understand a sign of peace. There was no acknowledgment.

Will kept a close watch on her. He went back to Dusty, rode him to within a few feet of the woman, and re-tied him to the scrub pine. The horse's eyes grew wide, and Dusty snuffled a few times at the smell of bear and blood. Lightning followed Will, growling as he approached the bear.

Watchful, Will walked over to the deer. Nearby, he saw an Indian man hidden behind a boulder, blood oozing from claw and bite marks around his head, face, and torso. He clutched a war club. Will had seen enough death to know this man was gone. Was he her husband? Near his other hand lay a revolver. Will picked it up and saw it was empty. He set it back down near the woman, just out of reach.

Will grabbed some cloth from his saddlebag and a bottle of whiskey. He knelt over her, pulling aside the sleeve of the ripped deerskin dress. Holding her wrist, he poured whiskey over the wound, wiping it with the cloth, and applied pressure until the bleeding stopped. After soaking another cloth with whiskey, Will wrapped the makeshift bandage around her wrist. Doctoring complete, he stood and waited, sweating and breathing hard, looking at her. Her black hair hung in braids at each side of her face. She appeared to be about eighteen years old, slim and pretty, with a straight, flat nose. Unsure what more to do, he shrugged and took a sip of the whiskey. The unaccustomed burn of the liquor in his throat made him cough.

Now what? he wondered. He couldn't just leave her there. But asking Dusty to carry them both in the heat was too much. Scanning on all sides, Will feared there might be other Indians nearby. He'd feel better when he could be on his way again. He scratched his head and wiped away trickling sweat from his forehead. What else could he do for her? He got his canteen from Dusty and wet a bandanna, wiping her face with the cool wetness. He tilted her head back to keep her breathing.

Her eyelids fluttered and then opened wide. She tried to reach for her knife with her good arm. Lightning let out a low growl. When Will pinned her arm to the ground, she struggled and spat at him. He released her, kicking the knife out of reach. She tried to rise, then fell back.

Will stood, backing up. He brought both hands in front of his chest, again making the sign for peace.

He waited to see if she would respond. For a minute, he wondered if she'd passed out again. Then she turned her head toward him, watching. He picked up the canteen and offered it to her. She took it and drank. Then she rolled to her side, facing him, and lay still again, exhausted. He pointed at the dead Indian, making the sign for dead.

She nodded and said, "*Deyaipe.*"

Will racked his brain for other signs he'd picked up at the Fort Leavenworth trading post. He had no idea what tribe this woman belonged to or why she would be out so far away from anyone. Was the man a would-be rescuer, her husband, or a captor? What should he do about her? How could he get her to let him help? Will looked around. Didn't she or the man on the ground have a horse?

Then he remembered and made the sign for a horse.

"*Bungu,*" she said and motioned toward the horizon, which Will took to mean that her horse had run off.

Looking at the horizon, he calculated there were about four hours of daylight left. He'd planned to make Fort Laramie today. However, he couldn't desert this wounded woman with an unloaded revolver and a knife, no horse, and no food. Perplexed, he looked at her again. He reached as if to touch her arm. Her face twisted in hate, and she pulled away.

Will again signed peace, beginning to feel helpless. She could not have weighed much over one hundred and twenty pounds. Maybe he should find her horse and lift her onto it. He pointed to the dead man and made the sign for husband. With great effort, she sat up and got her knees under her. She signed no. After resting, she stood. Eyes full of caution, she went to the bear. Though in obvious pain, she extended her arms to the sky and shuffled around the bear, singing in a low chant. After going around three times, she walked over to the knife. Will was alarmed as she picked it up, and he fingered the handle of his revolver. She ignored him and tried to skin the bear, keeping Will in her gaze. Grimacing in pain, she stopped. Her arm was bleeding again. He gave her more whiskey.

Will shook his head, deciding to leave her and let the whiskey take effect. He had to look about for the missing horse. Puzzling for a moment about making her understand, Will repeated the word he had heard her use, *"Bungu."* He pointed at her, then the horizon. He mounted Dusty and rode forward on the trail. Lightning trotted alongside. She did not look after him.

Will had gone about a mile when Lightning stiffened and looked ahead. He sniffed the ground, and Will saw hoofprints. Then he saw a pony off in the brush about fifty yards ahead, eating. There was a makeshift bag on its rump and a rawhide bridle on its head, hanging down to the dust. Dismounting and leading his horse, he edged toward it, humming a melody. He told Lightning to stay back, not wanting to spook the pony. Inching along, he was able to grasp the bridle and walk back to Dusty. Mounting again, he led the horse to the woman. Will was surprised to see her standing.

After securing her horse, he set about skinning and butchering the bear. Might as well use the meat. He built a small frame of saplings and stretched the hide on it to dry. Watching as she picked up the canteen to drink, he gathered some twigs and tinder and soon had a small blaze going. The woman leaned back against the tree, eyes closed. He guessed she didn't think he would attack her—or she was too worn out to care. Will put a few chunks of meat on a spit he'd fashioned. Maybe she'd feel stronger with some food.

The day was hot. Will stayed back from the fire, but his stomach growled at the agreeable odor of the roasting meat. Again, he puzzled about what to do with the woman. He had little experience with Indians at home in Kentucky. Once across the Missouri River, it was like another world.

He offered the woman meat and water. She hesitated, then accepted. He attempted to learn more about her with signing, but communication was difficult. As twilight set in, he gave up. He took the horses down to drink from the North Platte River. He removed a bedroll from his horse and hobbled him. He pantomimed sleep and lay down, with one end of the bridle tied to his bedroll. He kept both rifle and pistol near at hand, in case she should try to rob or harm him. He tossed and turned, dreaming again of being in Camp Douglas and watching his friend Archie die in battle.

When fingers of dawn stretched across the sky, he woke and stood in the chill air. The fire was out, and the woman sat on her haunches, watching him. He could not tell whether she had slept during the night. She offered him some raw meat and wrapped the other choice parts of the bear in leaves. Lightning walked over to her, whining, and she gave him a scrap of meat as well.

The time had come—there was no putting off deciding what to do about this woman. Will decided that she seemed capable enough. She seemed more energetic than yesterday, able to ride. He had no claim on her and knew nothing about her. He didn't know whether to trust her, beyond that, he had survived the night with his hair and possessions intact.

He accepted her gift of meat and the claws of the bear. Signing farewell, he mounted and started down the trail. Lightning whined as if conflicted, then trotted after him.

When he looked back, he saw she followed him on her pony at a short distance. It seemed he had acquired another companion.

CHAPTER THREE

Dove guided her mustang over the prairie, tagging along behind the white man. Her wounded arm hung at her side. She ignored the pain. Her motive in following was simple—she knew Cheyenne and Kiowa frequented the area, along with the occasional band of Omahas, all enemies of her tribe, the Shoshone. Her kidnapper, the dead brave behind the boulder, was Cheyenne. If caught alone on the prairie, the best she could hope for would be enslavement. She had escaped that and had no wish to risk it again. Traveling with the white man, she had at least a chance to get away while enemies were distracted killing him.

Now she could return to her tribe along the Wind River, a perilous journey. The thought of home made the pain in her arm worth enduring. The white man made her nervous; he could have killed her already, but so far, he seemed harmless. This puzzled her. Two years before, she had escaped the white soldiers on Bear River and made her way to Washakie's band. The prairie faded as she remembered.

The whites attacked on a cold winter morning when she was asleep. One moment she was dreaming in her tipi, the next chaos opened around her, with bullets flying, everyone screaming, the world gone insane. She crawled to her father, Lone Bear, keeping low. He grabbed his bow and arrows. They ran out of the tent, dodging as they heard the high whistle of incoming cannon shells from the bluff across the valley, sending hundreds of bullets streaking around them. Their friends and relatives fell, streams of blood, and cries of pain everywhere. Her aunt died defending her child. The snow turned red.

Dove's mother motioned her, and they ran after some of the other women, heading for the river. She looked back and saw her father wounded in the leg, struggling to follow them. Other warriors were still trying to mount a defense against the soldiers.

Then the whites began coming into the camp around the sides, killing everyone. Pistols roared, sabers slashed, people were falling everywhere. Her father crawled over to her as she and her mother slid down the thirty-foot embankment on deerskins to the river. Some of the women tried to swim across, holding on to their children through the icy water, but the soldiers shot them like ducks on a pond. Dove and her parents crawled into a cave under an overhang on the riverbank with a hot spring inside. Some other women were there, one holding a baby. The hot spring gave off steam that helped keep them warm.

They were quiet. Dove looked over at her father and saw he was wounded in the shoulder as well as the leg, a long bloody gash from a sword had cut open his deerskin vest. Her mother tried to stop the bleeding with snow.

After a time, the sound of firing began to diminish. They could hear soldiers shouting and hunting down survivors. The baby in the cave started to wail—what if the soldiers heard? The mother pulled down hard on the baby's head with a blanket to block the noise. The baby struggled to get free, and the mother pushed down, even more, stuffing the blanket into the baby's mouth. After a few minutes, the baby stopped struggling, lifeless, and limp.

When all was quiet, and the sun began to set, Dove ventured out of the cave, climbing up the riverbank. The soldiers were gone. The dead lay everywhere. Charred remains of tipis dotted the camp. She didn't even know where the wail came from. It started in the back of her throat and came out like the howl of a wolf. Bodies were strewn across the field, ringed by willows. Some had tried to run; others clutched whatever weapon they could find. Her friends, her family— the whites had spared no one.

The days after that blurred. There were no horses because the whites had taken them. One or two dogs were left, and it was hard to keep them from eating the dead. They needed to get away. What if the whites returned? She and her mother worked together to make a travois and hitched it to one of the larger dogs, placing her father on it, in the manner of her ancestors. She scavenged among the dead and came up with a pistol, bullets, a bow, and a few arrows. There was a little pemmican that had not burned. Her mother said they must go north, away from the whites. Washakie, her brother, had been here not many days before, for the Warm Dance, to beseech the coming of spring. Had the attack come then, thousands would have died. Now she hoped they could find Washakie and his band. A long, slow, frozen march lay in front of them with little hope and even less food.

The horror faded, and she came back to the present.

She considered this white man in front of her. From his signing, she understood his name to be *"Wilyam"* or something like that. Peculiar, but she had learned that white men's names often meant nothing. She'd told him hers, *Haiwi*, but didn't know if he understood. She pointed to a mourning dove when she told him. They were so ignorant, not knowing about Coyote or how to build a fire in the snow. The hairy white Mormons often came sniffing around her uncle's camp. She despised them and did not understand why her uncle tolerated them.

She kept an eye on the trail, in front and behind, as well as on the horizon and any rock formation, wary of possible enemies. Would the white man recognize a trap? She'd recovered her knife, but her revolver swayed between her breasts by its thong, unloaded.

Dove recognized the terrain. They were plodding along in the direction of the white man fort, Laramie. Dove guessed that they might get there sometime tomorrow at this pace if they did not run into any Cheyenne dog soldiers returning from a hunt. They would have to spend at least one more night on the open prairie.

As the sun began its downward trek, the white man stopped. She tensed, wondering what he saw, but then he took a long drink from the waterskin on his saddle and pulled a rifle out of its scabbard. He dismounted and balanced the rifle on a nearby boulder. She'd noticed he carried two rifles—he must be rich. What was the crazy white man doing? Did he see an enemy that she had missed?

She scanned the prairie. All she saw was an antelope, grazing about eight bow shots away.

He'll never hit it that far away, she thought. He'll wound it and let its spirit wander. It was a foolish waste of ammunition. Besides, they still had good bear meat. There was no need to hunt.

He hesitated, finger on the trigger, then broke his aim. He put the rifle back in the sheath and mounted. With a glance back at her, he continued.

After stopping for the night, the white man, Will, took Dove's revolver, loaded it, and kept it near his head. They had just lain down to sleep in the deepening twilight. The fire flickered between them. She was drifting off to sleep when she heard crackling twigs. At first, she ignored it, thinking the wood was popping in the fire. Then the horses began whickering, and the dog whined, then barked.

Grabbing her knife in her uninjured hand, she sat up and scanned the perimeter of the camp near the horses. She saw a shadowy figure crawling to where Will's horse stood.

She crawled to where Will lay and shook him. "*Tevuih!*" she whispered loud enough to make Will jump. Like a snake striking, Will grabbed his revolver and pushed her on her back, pointing it at her.

He must think she was the threat. They had seconds before the horses would be gone and they would be at the mercy of the thieves.

She dropped her knife and signed, "Enemy," pointing to the

horses. Will understood, signed that he would go right, she to the left. He gave her revolver back to her. She picked up her knife, and they circled toward the horses. Just as she saw a man untie the rope on Will's horse, Will fired. The dog streaked toward the thief, jumping and sinking his teeth into a shoulder. Dove found another brave unhobbling her pony, and she also shot but missed. Ignoring the pony for the moment, the brave dropped the halter and charged her, knife upraised. Dove fired again, this time hitting him full in the chest. The brave staggered but kept coming. The dog launched himself at the new assailant, but a kick sent him flying to the side.

The warrior twisted the pistol from her hand and brought his knife down fast. Terror sliced through her, but then the brave seemed to freeze. Dove's blade pierced his abdomen, and the dog sank his teeth into a leg. The knife sliced Dove's shoulder, and then her assailant toppled and fell as Will's bullet entered his brain. Blood spattered her. She started to feel weak and collapsed.

Throbbing pain shot down Dove's arm from shoulder to elbow. She attempted to rise but was too dizzy. She saw another bandage, higher on her arm. The white man was sitting close, standing guard. Judging from the sun, it must be almost the middle of the day. It was hot, and flies buzzed around her. She wondered why he was still there—didn't he know he was in danger? The braves that had tried to steal their horses no doubt had a camp and relatives not far away. Soon their families would search for them. She was too weak to fight if attacked. In his place, she would have left him. Why did he stay and protect her?

She passed in and out of consciousness. Her skin prickled with sweat, and she was aware of Will giving her water from his canteen and bathing her face with a wet cloth. After dark, he gave her some meat and dried bread to chew. She sat up, leaning on a boulder for support. She noticed he'd built no fire—maybe the white man wasn't foolish after all.

She slept in snatches, dreaming that Cheyenne surrounded their camp, but Coyote tricked them into not seeing them.

When morning came again, she ate and felt stronger. She stood on shaky legs and went down to the creek to wash and relieve herself. The white man didn't try to speak; instead, he tended the horses, with a constant eye on the skyline. The braves they'd killed lay where they had fallen. Vultures were beginning to circle above.

After some breakfast, Dove signed to the white man that they should go, face etched in pain as she made the movements. She told him she could ride. He tried to protest, but she made it clear that the braves on the ground and the vultures overhead placed them in danger.

Reluctant, he helped her onto her pony and mounted his horse. She struggled but stayed on as he walked the horses west, going in the creek to cover their tracks. Then, turning back to her, the white man gave her the reins and signed farewell, giving her a choice to go alone or follow.

Dove did not feel equal to being left alone. She followed him as he struck out northwest, heading for Fort Laramie. They made about five miles before dusk. Dove was sweating with heat, grateful for her companion's help getting down. He gave her meat and the dried bread that tasted like tanned hide.

She rested better that night. In the morning, they were on their way again. In the distance, she saw Fort Laramie and various tipis surrounding it, next to the Platte River.

CHAPTER FOUR

Will gazed in wonder at the number of tipis near the fort. Were the Indians so docile as to live in its shadow? After the attempted horse thievery two days ago, he wouldn't have believed it. Still, it seemed they could rest in safety at the fort with its soldiers. He looked back at Dove, slumped forward on her pony. Right now, the critical thing was to get her a doctor, bed rest, and food, in that order.

They wound through the Indians, with dogs and naked children staring at them. Will half wondered if the women would help his injured companion, but they seemed to ignore them. He reached the sentry's post and dismounted.

"Sir, this woman is injured, maybe near death. She needs a doctor."

"She your squaw?"

"What? No, she's just a woman in trouble. She decided to travel with me, maybe back to her people, I don't know—I don't speak her language. Then a few nights back, she was wounded by Indians trying to steal our horses. Please, Sergeant . . . She's hurt bad."

"Don't get so riled up. It's just a savage. If you didn't notice, we got plenty of 'em. One more or less ain't gonna matter."

Will's face reddened. He clenched his fists, wanting to flatten the lout. He shouted, "She's a human being. She's in pain and suffering. If it were your sister or mother, you wouldn't be standing there—you'd be running for the sawbones."

"Right. But my sister ain't no dirty Injun."

"Soldier, I want to see the doctor or your commanding officer," Will said in his best lieutenant's voice.

"Suit yerself. But ain't no squaw coming on the post without the commander's say so. Considering he just lost a nephew to Red Cloud's bunch a few days ago, I wouldn't hold out much hope."

The sergeant turned and bellowed, "Billings! Man here wants

to see General Connor. And find the sawbones—if he ain't drunk."

As Will began to give up hope, a burly man with a thin, straight mouth and beak-like nose wandered over to the gate. He squinted at Dove, then turned to the sergeant.

"Sergeant, if you value your stripes, you'd best get two men and carry that squaw to my quarters. She's Shoshone, or I'm a groundhog. Unless you want all her relatives hunting your blood, you'd best mind what I say."

The sergeant looked startled and then said, "Well, sure, Old Gabe! I'd no idea she was important."

An officer with a star on his shoulder came up. "What's the trouble here? Can't you stand simple guard duty, soldier?"

Gabe raised a hand. "Hold on, General Connor! I advise you to make this squaw comfortable and see to her. You don't want her relatives thinking you're the one to blame for her death."

Connor turned to Gabe. "I've fought Shoshone before, maybe some of her kin. I don't much care what her relations think—I've killed enough of them."

Looking back at the sergeant, he said, "But if Gabe thinks she's important, it's good enough for me. He knows these people better'n anybody. Sergeant, get her a billet and make her comfortable. See that Gabe has anything he needs."

Billings returned and, seeing General Conner, saluted. "Sir! Private Billings is reporting. Sir, the sawbones is drunk again. Begging your pardon, I wouldn't let him operate, even on her."

Gabe spoke up. "Never mind, Private. I've fixed many a wound. I'll take care of her. Get me some strong whiskey. Somebody check the sawbone's stores and see if he has arrowroot. Get her down."

As the men moved toward her, Dove seemed ready to fall off but kicked the pony, and it moved forward, knocking the men over. Gabe caught the makeshift bridle and stopped the pony. He addressed her in Shoshone, his tone soft and comforting. Dove relaxed.

The men offered assistance again. This time she slid off the horse into their arms, and Will followed as they carried her to Gabe's quarters.

Will fell into an uneasy sleep. About midnight, hearing shots and a bugler blowing the charge, he woke and jerked upright. He jumped to his feet, drawing a pistol, but no one was there. A dream. Sweating, he tried to focus on the dark reality of the billet around him.

He lit a lamp and tried to read his Bible. But the scenes of David and Jonathan going up against the Philistines just brought back the war. Somehow he'd lost God, his anchor. Maybe that's what the search was all about. He was alone, and he needed something, someone, a foundation.

Shaking, he decided to go over to Gabe's cabin to see how his companion fared.

He knocked on the door and heard nothing. The door was flung open, and Gabe appeared to the side of it, pistol cocked. Will held up his hands, palms out. Gabe let his arm fall and holstered his gun. He motioned for Will to enter.

"How is she?"

"Not good. But I think she'll make it. She's been asleep ever since she got here."

"Did she tell you what happened?"

"No, but I can guess near enough. The country's alive with Cheyenne and Arapaho, either of which would kill her on sight or take her for a slave. She told me her name, Dove, *Haiwi*. And that she's niece to Chief Washakie."

"And so?"

"And so you better hope she lives lest her uncle decides to blame you for her death. The soldiers would be lucky to find enough of your scalp for a brave to wear."

"How is it you speak her language?"

"Allow me to introduce myself—I'm Jim Bridger." He grinned and made a mock bow. "Folks around here call me Old Gabe. Had me a Shoshone wife awhile back. Me and Washakie, chief of the Eastern Shoshone, been friends for years. Reckon this gal musta come back to Washakie after I left—her ma was with the Western Shoshone band, wiped out at Bear River."

"What happened? To your wife, I mean."

"She died birthing a young'un."

"I'm sorry."

"It happens a lot. Now I work for the Army or the wagon trains going west."

"I feel kinda responsible for her. She got hurt defending our horses and me. If she hadn't heard them sneaking up on us, I'd be dead."

"New in this country, are you?"

"Yes, sir."

"Well, you picked the wrong time to come. If I were headed back to Leavenworth, I'd take you along. Greenhorn like you got no business out here with the way things are."

"With the way things are?"

Gabe sighed. "The Army is about to mount an expedition into Powder River country. They're aiming to scout out fort locations and kill Indians—no quarter. Red Cloud's Sioux, the Arapahoe, and the Cheyenne are not going to roll over."

"I came looking for peace, maybe do a little trapping."

Gabe laughed. "You sure know how to pick 'em. Trapping's done—no beaver left. This here country's 'bout as calm as a bull bison fightin' a grizzly. If you come to find peace, you're out of luck. And after the expedition makes ten miles west, I wouldn't bet a lame mule on you making it back east to civilization with your life."

"I fought in the war . . . I can handle myself."

"Maybe you did. But what you don't know about Indians would fill that entire prairie out there."

"What about all the Indians in front of the fort?"

"You mean them Brulé Sioux? They call 'em the Laramie Loafers. Spotted Tail's bunch. They gave up fighting white men. But they wouldn't mind stealing her." He gestured at Dove.

"I was planning to go farther west, into the mountains."

Gabe shook his head. "You ought to go home. Wherever home is, wait for a troop or wagon train headed back east, and stay with them. That would be your best chance. I've been in the mountains nigh on forty years. You'd be lucky to last a week on your own. If you fight well, you might die fast. That's the best you could hope for."

Will stuck his jaw out, stubborn. Unbidden, the image of Lydia's frightened face as he pointed a pistol at her came again. Will's determination hardened.

"I'm not going back."

"Suit yourself. If you're determined to go west, talk to Connor. He might let you join the expedition if you fought like you say. You'd at least last longer that way."

Will looked over at Dove. She said something delirious in her fevered sleep. He noticed Gabe had tied her arm close to her body so that she couldn't thrash around. He watched her breasts rise and fall and thought for a moment how beautiful she was. Pushing that away, he asked, "What about her?"

"What about her? She knows better how to travel than you do. In a few days, the expedition will start. She won't be well enough to travel. I might persuade Connor to let her stay here until spring. She'll have to make her way west to her people. She ought to be well enough to travel by then."

"And if I go on my own?"

"Leave me a letter for your next of kin so's I can tell them what happened to you."

Reveille woke Will with a start. The military alarm had him thinking himself back in Morgan's Camp Charity, Kentucky, before the war. When he realized his surroundings, his heart stopped hammering. Lighting a lamp, he reached into his saddlebag and pulled out his Bible. He spent the next hour, combing the pages of scripture and praying, looking for guidance. In Proverbs, he found the verse about the Lord turning the heart of the king any way he wished. Today Will felt like this was for him—he would go to Connor and seek permission to accompany the expedition. If the officer had doubts, Will would challenge the troop's best marksman to a match for the privilege of going along on the trip.

He pulled on his boots, tidied himself, and walked to the commander's office.

"Will Crump, reporting. The commander will want to see me."

A bored private looked up and just motioned him in.

Connor glanced at him. "Yes, what is it? You're the one that brought in the squaw yesterday."

"Yes, Sir. And I'd like to see that she gets back to her tribe."

Connor snorted, glaring at Will. "You'd have done better to have left her on the prairie. Now you've given me another headache. If she does get well—and with Gabe tending her, she will—she'll be taken captive by the Sioux if she ventures more than a hundred yards from this fort. Even a Crow warrior might take a fancy to her. Leave it. She's not worth your trouble."

"I plan to go west into the mountains. I want to request joining the expedition I hear you're leading, at least part of the way. Gabe says her people are in the mountains in northern Wyoming territory."

"Suicidal, are you?"

"No, sir."

Exasperated, Connor flicked at the pages on his desk. "Look, son. I don't know what you think you're doing out here, but I don't need one more greenhorn to protect."

"I can fight."

Connor looked amused. "You don't look old enough. Fought in the war, did you?"

"Yes, Sir. A lieutenant. Sharpshooter."

Connor raised his eyebrows, stretching his full muttonchop mustache. "Sharpshooter, you say? Berdan?"

"No, Sir. I wore the gray."

"Another reason to deny you. 'Spect you're just going to join the other Rebs in Idaho."

"No, Sir. I don't mean trouble for anyone. But if, as you say, the country out there is hostile, you might need someone who can shoot."

Seeing Conner's skeptical look, Will hesitated, thinking of his episodes. He pushed that aside and said, "Tell you what . . . I'll challenge your best shot to a match. I'll use my Sharps; he can use whatever he likes. Range six hundred yards. If he wins, I'll take the next stage or transport back to Fort Leavenworth. If I win, you take me along. Five shots."

Connor chuckled. "Pretty sure of yourself, aren't you? All right, this sounds worth seeing. Noon today, west side of the fort. Dismissed."

Will worried walking back to his cabin—what if the world swam again when he fired? But what choice did he have? He needed safe-conduct—it was that or go home, exposing his shame to his family and putting them in danger.

The crowd gathered outside the fort north of the bakery to see the spectacle. Will was glad they'd agreed to Old Gabe as the judge; he figured to get a fair shake from him. Will checked his rifle and his ammunition, then walked over to his handlebar-mustached opponent.

"Figured I might as well introduce myself. I'm Will Crump," he said, sticking out a hand.

"Sergeant Hurst—Bill Hurst, Company E. I hear you were a Johnny Reb." He ignored Will's hand.

"I was. Just a citizen like anyone else now."

"I was in the unit assigned to track Morgan in the war. Lots of my friends died. Maybe we've shot against each other before, but not at targets." He smiled, but the smile held neither friendship nor kindness.

"Maybe so. I'm sure you did your duty, as I did mine. But the war is over. And I'm just looking for peace, safe passage to the mountains. No offense, but I have to beat you to get there."

"We'll see about that!" Hurst snarled. "You picked a strange place to look for peace. Just fought a battle at Platte River Bridge, outnumbered ten to one. Your scalp will be on a lodgepole before the month is out."

Will decided to retreat for the time being. No use getting worked up and missing his shots. He was nervous enough already. How would he last for five shots? He plugged the cotton he'd brought in his ears. He watched as Old Gabe set the target and walked back toward them.

"All right!" Gabe quieted the crowd. "Gonna have us a little shooting match. Each feller takes five shots, no time limit. Bull's-eye is fifty, each ring outside that ten less. High score wins. Gun jams or gets fouled, you forfeit. Got me a six-cent piece here. Johnny Reb, you call it." He flipped the coin in the air.

"Heads," said Will.

"You come and look, Sergeant."

Hurst looked on the ground. "Tails, looks like to me."

Gabe looked and nodded. "All right, Sergeant. You're up first."

Hurst loaded his own Sharps rifle. Will noted it was longer and bulkier than his. He adjusted his sight. Maybe this guy wouldn't be so easy to beat.

Hurst took his time, fired, reloaded, and fired with precision born of practice. Will covered his ears to deaden the sound further. He couldn't resist watching, though. The report of the rifle made him jump, but with it muffled, he did not experience the vertigo that had troubled him. The target was ten inches in diameter. Hurst seemed very calm, not nervous at all. But then, what did he have to lose beyond reputation?

Old Gabe sauntered out to retrieve the target and put up a new one. Another soldier accompanied him from Hurst's company to be sure all was fair.

When he returned, he looked over the target, then handed it first to Will, then Hurst.

Holding up the target, Gabe announced to the crowd, "We have two in the inner ring for forty apiece, three in the next ring for thirty apiece. Total score: one hundred seventy for Sergeant Hurst." Turning to him, he said, "Good shooting, sir!"

Gabe nodded at Will, who loaded and took nervous aim. Out of the corner of his eye, he saw Dove off to his right, standing with effort. What was she doing here? What was she even doing up and about? No time for that. Concentrate!

His first shot was off, no better than the third ring, maybe even the fourth. Concentrate! Pull the lever, cock, aim! No prizes for speed here—only accuracy. No one is shooting back. Breathe, then hold it, release. Again. After the next release, squeeze.

His next shot was better. Repeat twice more, and then the final shot. It all came down to this shot. In the war, he hadn't more than a few seconds, not much time to think, no time to be nervous. Someone in the crowd shouted about the Johnny Reb being afraid. Will forced himself to breathe, to do what he knew, not to think about Dove or home or the war, the faces of the men he'd killed. Breathe out, squeeze—and the last shot fired.

Gabe retrieved the target and passed it to Hurst, whose eyes bulged a bit. He started shaking his head. Then Gabe handed it to Will. One in the third ring—his first. Three in the second ring . . . and one bull's-eye!

"The Johnny Reb scores two hundred!" Gabe thundered. A few feeble whistles of "Dixie" went up, then a rebel yell from some of the galvanized Yankees.

Connor came up to Will.

"Well, Johnny Reb, you won. I've not seen shooting like it. But I'm not sure I'm doing you a favor, letting you tag along. We're going to kill every Indian we find, 'cept maybe the little kids."

Under Gabe's doctoring, Dove improved. Will entered Gabe's cabin, looking for him. Gabe wasn't there. He found Dove building a fire in the Franklin stove. Will watched her for a moment until she turned to him, realizing his presence. He signed to her but found she still had difficulty responding due to her injured arm. She turned back to the stove, ignoring him.

He picked up an armful of kindling, bringing it to the stove. When he got too close, Dove spat and shouted at him. He put the wood by the stove and backed off, stumbling over a stool in his haste.

When Gabe was around, she chattered and sometimes scolded, making Gabe laugh. She seemed fine with Gabe. Why did she show Will hostility?

With nothing better to do, Will sat at the table, read his Bible, prayed, and thought about the upcoming expedition. He figured he might as well wait until Gabe came back. Maybe Dove would get used to him. He'd been spending time with Gabe whenever he could, trying to learn bits of Dove's Shoshone language and coaxing her with English words. Will learned haa meant yes. He tried words he'd learned and sign language with Dove, but she either laughed or remained hostile.

What was it about her that made him want to help her? He guessed he'd always been a sucker for a girl in trouble. It was tempting to give up and leave her to Gabe. Yet if he were going to survive in this country, he'd have to learn about Indians.

He still felt responsible for her. In the night, when he wasn't fighting the dreams of the past, he had to admit to himself that she was attractive. Was that it? She was a stranger—did he have any business thinking of her that way? Her hostility just made her more of a puzzle—one he wanted to solve. She seemed alone in the world; maybe the two of them could be alone together.

Will had an idea. Maybe, just maybe if he could make her laugh, she would see that he meant her no harm.

He thought of the games he used to play with his sister Lydia when she was little. Thinking of Lydia made his heart ache, but he pushed that aside. He got down on all fours and pretended to be Lightning, barking, scratching, and whining. The noise attracted her attention. She might think he was crazy, but what did he have to lose?

Just as it seemed he was making progress—she wasn't being hostile or ignoring him, and she even smiled a little—a girl with long brown braids flung open the door of Gabe's cabin. Dove jumped backward, moving closer to her knife, lying on the bed. Will glanced over at the intruder, brow furrowing in annoyance. The intruder was less than five feet tall, slim figure, maybe fourteen years old, Will guessed. Her green eyes darted to Dove. Will tried to sign to Dove, to reassure her. On seeing the strange pantomime of signs and hearing the half-English, half-Shoshone gibbering, the girl burst out laughing.

"You two should do a show," she said, still laughing. "Is Gabe around?"

Will glanced at Dove and saw her mouth turn down, her arms folded. The muscles in her neck tensed.

"Haven't seen him—I was looking for him myself. This is Dove. I'm Will. What's your name?"

"Oh, sorry, manners. I'm Clarissa Cochran. My pa is first sergeant with Company E."

"Pleased to meet you, Clarissa. I'll tell Gabe you stopped by."

"Thanks." Hesitating, she said, "Could you tell her I meant no harm? It's just that you look so funny doing all that motioning."

"It's sign language. I don't speak her language well yet, and she doesn't speak much English. You can tell her yourself if you want. Just hold your hands in front of you, clap them together, and hold them for a minute. That tells her you're a friend."

Clarissa looked hesitant but then did as Will instructed. Dove glanced around, then responded with the same sign.

"Don't tell my pa. He wouldn't like me talking to an Indian. I should get back home . . . Ma will wonder where I am." She turned and left.

Two days later, Will was walking across the parade ground when he heard bugles. Looking across the river, he saw a column of soldiers with Gabe riding off to the left side. A dust cloud rose behind the horses as they approached the river. Will watched as Gabe swam his horse across, jouncing as they came up the bank on the fort side. The sentries moved aside to let them enter.

Turning to the private cleaning the cannon on the parade ground, Will asked, "So where are they coming from? I've missed Gabe the last couple days—no one seemed to know where he'd gone."

"Oh, they knew right enough. Just that Conner don't want nobody saying they been scouting Injuns."

"Why? Are they worried about an attack on the fort?"

The private grinned. "Naw, nothing like that. Ain't no group of Injuns going to attack this here fort, 'long as I keep the cannons working. Rumor has it Conner's to punish them—and he's more'n happy to oblige."

"Punish them? For what?"

"Ever since the gold rush started in '49, more folks moving along the trails to California, Oregon, Colorado—wherever there's a rumor of gold. Injuns don't like it much. They attack the wagon trains, so the Army defends them. "

"The more that come, the worse it gets?"

"Naw, the Injuns won't last. They'll corral them and ship them off. Then the land can be used by civilized folk to farm. You could claim yourself some land if'n you swallow the dog, give allegiance to the USA."

"Thanks, but I grew up farming. I'm looking for a simpler way. Besides, claiming someone else's land doesn't seem right."

"Suit yourself, Reb."

Will visited Dove over the next two days, making sure she had food and that someone was tending her. He noticed a change, a thaw in her attitude toward him. She made an effort to speak English and seemed respectful. Will wasn't sure what to attribute the change to, but he was glad of it. Still, he supposed it didn't matter much if he split off from the expedition and did not return. Will packed his gear, checked his rations and ammunition. Dove watched, showing occasional interest in his preparations. Connor was unwilling to let Dove come with them, suspicious that she would warn their enemies—and besides, in the heat of battle, she'd just get shot.

Will heard a loud commotion on the parade ground. Troopers were mounting up, hitching up two mountain howitzers. Drums were beating, bugles blowing, everyone rushing to prepare. Will went to the door. To his surprise, he saw Connor order the howitzers pointed at his men of the Sixteenth Kansas. There was a lot of shouting, but he was too far away to understand. It was clear that there was some contention. Then the Kansas men got up and fell in line.

Will went back to packing.

Gabe came in. "General's 'bout ready to mount up. Some of the Kansans want to go home. They say their enlistment will be up before this trip is over. You don't have to do this, you know."

"Yes, I do. I did the match to gain a spot. Everybody tells me to go with a group—so this is it. Been looking at maps, and I think when Conner turns back, I'll branch off toward your old place, Fort Bridger. Maybe I could have a little cabin, hunt for the Army. I'd appreciate it if you see that Dove gets home after you come back."

"Ain't no guarantees on any of us coming back. If I do, I'll try to see she gets back to her people. I owe Washakie a visit anyhow."

Dove took Will's arm.

"Do you have to go? I hear they are just going to kill Indians. Do you want to do that?"

"Well, no. But you're safe here, I think. I . . . I like you. I feel responsible for you. But Gabe will get you home. I need to go on with what I came for."

Will grabbed his gear and headed for the stables, followed by Gabe. Lightning trotted after them. He threw a saddle on Dusty, mounted, and trotted to the parade ground.

Connor addressed the commanders and the Pawnee and Omaha scouts under the command of Captain Frank North.

"Gentlemen, we are going to war. This expedition is to punish any hostiles in our way. There will be three prongs for the expedition: one ranging far north, Colonel Cole's coming up from Nebraska, and ours taking the southern route. We will find the savages and destroy them. Any Arapaho, Sioux, or Cheyenne that we encounter younger than twelve years old is to live. The rest we will kill. There's always hope for the young ones. Colonel Walker, you will advance north to the Black Hills, engaging any hostiles in your path, then rendezvous with us on the Powder River. I've just received word by telegraph of a supply train that will come to supply this post and any new forts we build, led by Lieutenant Colonel James Sawyer. Though not a part of our expedition, I'm sure receiving the supplies before winter will be most welcome. The Omaha and Pawnee scouts will stay with my command. Any questions, gentlemen? Bugler, sound advance!"

CHAPTER FIVE

Dove watched Gabe and Will go. She was tired, and her arm ached. She knew she wasn't up to traveling alone yet. With Gabe gone, she felt isolated; no one here knew her language or culture. No one cared about her. The chief of the white men was leaving too. Who knew what the new chief would do with her? She recognized Conner's name as the perpetrator of the Bear River Massacre, where he and his soldiers had murdered her family. She wanted to put an arrow in his back, but she wouldn't dare. They would hang her for sure.

Gabe was so different from Conner—he bridged the two worlds. Gabe understood about the Coyote and Wolf spirits, how Wolf was the helper and Coyote the trickster. Gabe talked almost as one of her people. Will was a puzzle to her—he was white, but he'd been nothing but kind. He cared about her welfare. But why? She allowed herself to think of him as handsome but then pushed that away. He was white. That made him an enemy, or at least not to be trusted.

To get back to her people, she needed to travel before the snows. The problem would be the Sioux and Cheyenne around the fort and Arapaho to the north.

Dove stood, forcing herself to balance and stay upright. Flexing her arm made her feel a little dizzy.

I'm in no shape to travel, much less fight, she thought. Dove wondered what had happened to her revolver . . . and her horse. She must see to that. Would the white men steal it? Why wouldn't they? She was in their power. They'd accuse her of stealing it if she were to ride out of the fort.

Just as she started to feel hungry and wondered what she could do for food now that Gabe and Will had left, she heard a knock at the door. She slipped a horn knife on a leather lanyard around her neck and down her dress to conceal it. If the white men came to hurt her, she'd fight or at least try to resist. Opening the door, Dove saw the white girl, Clarissa, who used to come and visit Gabe.

"I came to see how you're doing," she said. "Gabe" was followed by words she didn't understand, and then Clarissa indicated a knapsack at her feet, picking it up to offer it to Dove.

Dove understood about half of what the girl said, but she knew the sack was for her, and the girl mentioned Gabe, so she figured it was all right to take it. She signed her thanks, not knowing whether the girl would understand.

They stood looking at each other, not knowing what to do or say. Clarissa reached up and took a decorative pin from her hair. She pressed it into Dove's hand with a smile and turned to go with a wave.

Dove was surprised. She did not expect kindness from the white girl. Gabe said her father was one of the soldiers, and Dove knew what to expect from them. Visions of death and blood arose unbidden, hiding in the cave, waiting for death.

Without Gabe's protection, she felt deserted, but now maybe she had an ally. If she could gain enough strength, get some food, her horse, and weapons, perhaps she would have a chance to get home. She had not tracked how many sleeps she'd traveled with the Cheyenne brave who'd kidnapped her—there had been no reason to mark a stick. She knew, however, that it must have been at least two moons. With more Cheyenne and Sioux to dodge, she must start soon, or Washakie would be south in the valleys and harder to find.

Dove opened the knapsack and found bannocks, dried venison jerky, a round metal canteen, and chokecherries. She was astonished. The girl's mother, perhaps? However it came, Wolf was watching out for her, thwarting Coyote's tricks.

She ate little. Exhausted, she pulled the latch string inside for safety, fell back on the bed, and slept.

For several days, she ventured out only at night to use the privy. She hadn't grown accustomed to it and hated the stench, but she knew among the whites there was no other choice. She looked forward to Clarissa's regular visits, even though it meant starting over to teach someone to communicate with her. She found that the signing was sometimes painful, but she figured she must push through the pain and use the arm or find it growing useless.

Dove's English improved, though she understood more than she could speak. She gained useful information from the girl, who chattered on every imaginable topic. She learned that at least a third of the soldiers were without horses, and horses were much desired. Dove guessed her chance of getting her horse returned without a fight was non-existent.

After a week, she decided she must venture out in the daytime. It appeared that the soldiers had forgotten about her. The fort had no walls. Instead, there was a wide trench around it with the river on two sides. Walking with no seeming purpose, she ambled toward the corral on the northeast end of the fort. There weren't many animals, perhaps twenty horses in all. At night, it should be possible to steal one. She saw her pony, mingled in with the other horses; the whites thought it too small for anything but a packhorse. They didn't recognize that it would be running and loping when their big mounts were dead from exhaustion on the prairie.

"Hey, you! Squaw! What're you doing over here?"

Startled, Dove saw a greasy, unkempt soldier advancing on her.

"I was looking at my horse," she managed.

"Your horse? You're not supposed to be on the post—wait, ain't you that squaw Gabe brought in half-dead a few weeks back?"

Encouraged, she said, "That's right."

He laughed, showing yellowed teeth. "Well, that doesn't change nothing. You prob'ly stole the horse anyway. Government property now—you can even see the US brand on the little runt. Too small to ride, 'cept maybe for a squaw like you. Say, now that Gabe and that other feller's gone, you might be wanting some company." He started to reach for her, but Dove sprang back. "No need to be unfriendly-like. You must be wanting a real man by now." He reached for her again.

Dove backed into the corral post. Cornered, she reached up with her good arm and pulled up the leather thong that held her knife. Armed, she crouched and waited.

The man laughed again. He wasn't afraid. He tried to grab the wrist that held the knife. Dove slashed across his palm, moving sideways a step.

"Hey! You worthless little wildcat! I oughta . . ." He moved toward her again as if to pin her arms to her sides.

Her mind saw again the soldiers at Bear River, death all around her.

Dove knew she dared not let him capture her; she was wobbling a bit already. With all the strength she had left, she made an underhanded stab at the soldier's belly, just above the belt. He tottered backward in surprise . . . and they both fell.

When Dove awoke, she was in the guardhouse. Bars on the windows and a locked door told her that she was in trouble. She had blood on her clothes, her head throbbed, and she wasn't sure she could walk, but she tried. She made it to the window and grabbed the bars. Outside, all looked normal, people moving about their business. She heard something at the door and walked back to the rude bunk.

She heard Clarissa telling the guard, "Someone's got to take care of her. Now out of the way! Or I'll tell my daddy you were bothering me."

The door opened, and Clarissa came in carrying a clean dress and bannock cakes.

"Thought you might wake up hungry."

"How long have I been here?"

"Oh, a day, day, and a half. They found you and Private Buckman on the ground by the corral, both unconscious. Looks like Buckman will live, more's the pity. But he says you just attacked him, which is why you're in here. Why would you do that?"

"He . . . he tried to grab me. He was going to . . ." Dove trailed off.

"I see. He's been a problem with other women. The thing is, because you're an Indian and no one saw, it's your word against his. And they won't believe you."

"What will they do?"

"Well, for now, they're just holding you until General Conner returns. But that could be a few weeks yet or a few days. No one knows. Everyone's nervous about Indians right now, which doesn't help you."

"I need to get strong and leave. The snow will come soon. I must reach my people."

She saw Clarissa's surprise. "My ma is on your side, thinks Buckman is to blame. But the men . . . I wouldn't count on going anywhere soon. My pa hates Indians, but he figgers because you're a woman, you need someone, so he's letting me visit. How's the arm?"

Dove flexed her left arm, wincing with the effort. "Still hurts to move it much. But it hasn't turned green or black."

"I can bring some extra food to help you get stronger, but I can't promise much more than that. They won't let me bring in whiskey. Some of the soldiers don't think I should come at all, that you'd hurt me."

Dove smiled without warmth. "No, I won't hurt you. I'm able to walk, not much more. You've been a good friend."

"Well, I should go. They've got you charged with attempted

murder. Try and think of anyone who might have seen what happened. When the trial comes, you'll need them."

Day spilled into day, each one long, tedious, and sizzling. Dove slept much of the time and grew stronger. Clarissa would visit every three or four days, once even bringing hot stew. Dove looked forward to her visits, always afraid her father would forbid her. Nights began to grow colder, and Dove missed the buffalo robe she would have had at home. Flies were a problem, with no campfire smoke to send them away.

The cell smelled disgusting. She had no way to bathe, and the chamber pot sat for two or three days at times before two soldiers entered to empty it, holding their noses. She watched the trees beginning to lose their leaves and turn colors.

What if General Conner did not return? What if they hanged her when he did?

CHAPTER SIX

Will rode near the rear of the column, staying out of General Conner's path. Lightning trotted alongside Dusty. Will couldn't explain his devotion, but he was glad of it. His goal was to go with the soldiers long enough to clear hostile Sioux territory. He hoped to find a quiet lake somewhere in the mountains, where he could hunt, fish, and maybe grow a garden, living a solitary life for a time. He could pray, find God, and be at peace. He didn't know what came next, and right now, he didn't care.

His conscience bothered him when he thought of Dove, but why should he be concerned about her? He'd gotten her help. Gabe would return to the fort, and he had connections with her people. As for General Conner, Will wanted no part of his revenge killings, his vow to kill every Indian they encountered. He'd defend himself or someone threatened, but no more. Will had shown himself plenty stubborn in the last war. Conner wasn't going to succeed in changing his mind.

Now mid-August, the summer was waning fast as they journeyed west and north from the fort. Everyone was jumpy, expecting any moment to round the bend and find a Sioux village, or worse, a Sioux war party.

Will had his own tent but decided to seek Gabe's fire that night. He set a snare and, after catching two rabbits, brought those along to contribute to the pot.

"Evening, Gabe. Thought I'd bring some grub."

"Obliged. Will, sit, have some coffee, pull up a rock."

"I wondered . . . what about the Shoshone? I want to go over around Wind River, help Dove get home. Should I expect trouble?"

"Depends. It's like asking a woman to dance—depends on her mood. Striking off on your own like you're thinking . . ." Gabe shook his head. "Winter's coming up, and you'll starve or freeze if you don't get to be a pincushion for arrows."

"You don't think I should have come?"

"Nope. But you're here now, and you bought your place with that shooting. The problem is the Sioux, Blackfeet, or Pawnee would have your skull bashed in before you knew they were there."

"Don't you think it's possible to make friends with the Indians? Why does there have to be war?"

"Suppose a woman's husband promises to come right home after work, but night after night, he goes drinking and whoring. Her little sister gets a proposal of marriage from a nice feller, but she saw what happened to her older sister, so she turns it down. Not unreasonable, right? How's she to know that her beau is honorable, different from her sister's husband? Same thing here. The Shoshone see a white man, they don't know if he's good or bad. After the Bear River Massacre, they're going to assume bad and ask questions later, 'specially the ones around Fort Hall. They're defending their home and families. The army has broken treaty after treaty. Why should the Shoshone trust them?"

"But they trust you . . ."

"I've risked my scalp to earn it. If you want to live at peace among them, you'll have to prove yourself."

"How?"

"Being a good hunter, a square dealer, and not afraid of Beelzebub hisself. And realizing most tribes don't have a rigid leadership structure, the army gets that wrong all the time. Be good to the land, don't hunt more'n you need to eat, use what the good Lord gives you—all of it."

The next morning as Will was finishing his coffee, Gabe came over.

"The Pawnee think they've seen sumpin' ahead. Me and one of the officers gonna take a look-see. Wanna come?"

Will yawned and rubbed his eyes. "Sure, Gabe. Expect trouble?"

"No, but General Conner seems determined to look for it."

"I'll be saddled up and ready in five minutes."

Gabe strode off in the direction of the horse picket line.

They rode to the northwest, angling back and forth between the trees to the top of the next hill. Will and Captain Palmer listened and watched as Gabe told them how to track Indians, how to tell the moccasins of one tribe from another, and other tips from his decades of experience in the mountains.

At the top of the rise, they stopped. Palmer took out his field glasses and began scanning the distant hills. Squinting, Gabe looked far away using just his eyes. Will only saw bluffs and forest. They heard the occasional chop of an ax—Conner had decided to build a stockade here in the wilderness, naming it after himself.

Palmer lowered his glasses. Will could detect nothing. Lightning sat next to Dusty, whining.

"Looks peaceful enough," said Palmer.

"Did you see? Off to the left there, just over that second ridge," said Gabe.

Palmer raised his glasses, looking again. "That must be six, maybe eight miles away. No, I don't see anything. You?" he said, turning to Will.

"No, sir, can't say I do. But if Gabe sees something . . ."

"Smoke, you fool greenhorns, smoke. Several columns of it. Looks to me like a village, prob'ly up there near where the Tongue intersects that little creek from the north."

Will strained his eyes but could see nothing—just trees, rocks, barren land. Palmer looked at Will and shrugged as Gabe kept his eyes trained to the distance.

"Uh, sure, Gabe. Whatever you say. Smoke." Palmer winked at Will.

"Will, you ride back to camp. Get General Conner up here. He wants some action; he's about to have it. Send some of them Pawnee back with him. And tell him to lay off those axes—they make enough noise to telegraph President Johnson."

Will was used to courier duty and turned his horse to camp, pushing Dusty to a fast walk down the steep, rocky slope.

Half an hour later, he returned with Connor and three Pawnee scouts.

"What's all the fuss, Gabe?" said Connor.

"Well, sir, that's why I asked you to come. Palmer, let General Conner see your glasses."

Connor took them, scanned the horizon, and shook his head. "I see nothing alarming."

Palmer grinned. "Gabe here's just funning us greenhorns. Says there's smoke over those ridges—a whole village. Good joke, Gabe!"

Gabe said nothing, lifted his eyes toward heaven, and took another plug of tobacco. Will had a distinct feeling it was not a joke.

"Yes, well, uh, can't be too careful, I guess. There's no smoke, but perhaps you'd ask these Pawnee gentlemen to make sure, go down a bit closer," said Conner. "Report back to me. Good day."

Gabe said a few words, and the Pawnee moved in the direction he indicated, disappearing in the forest.

"We'll circle east, to make sure them in the village aren't already spying on us, and then back to camp," said Gabe.

"Sure thing," said Palmer, holding back a chuckle.

Will brought up the rear, following the other two. He checked his pistol and tested his stirrups, making sure the girth was tight enough. He'd come off a horse in rough country before and had no desire to repeat the experience.

They wound through the warm August morning but saw no signs. Hours later, after a cold lunch and a short rest, they saw the Pawnee return. They went straight to Gabe, talking and gesturing.

Conner approached. "Well?"

Gabe smirked. "Sir, the Pawnee report a village of Arapaho ahead, just north of the junction of the two cricks. They can't say how many warriors, but they guess about one hundred fifty ponies. Maybe one hundred tipis."

Conner's eyebrows rose. He turned to Palmer, whose mouth was making an O of astonishment. "Captain, assemble the company commanders, my tent, ten minutes."

"Sir, is that necessary? One company of cavalry should handle the village."

Gabe snorted. "You best take all ninety of your Pawnee and every trooper you have. You're gonna need 'em."

Conner turned to Will. "What about you, Mr. Crump? With your rifle up on a hill above the village, you might save some lives."

Will's mouth set hard in a straight line. "No, sir. If you choose to attack a village that is not threatening this command, that is your affair. I'll watch the horses, tend the wounded. I'll save lives that way."

"Yellow belly rebel!" shouted a nearby soldier.

Conner turned away in disgust.

"Very well. Captain Palmer, the commanders."

Gabe talked to Captain North, who was in charge of the Pawnee scouts.

By dusk, the troopers were moving out. Gabe had agreed to lead them. When Will saw the mountain howitzers moving toward the sleeping village, his stomach tightened and he stuffed his ears with cotton.

The morning dawned foggy and cold. Gabe had cautioned everyone against fires and allowed no reveille. Will worked with a medical orderly, a corporal, to prepare tents and cots for the anticipated wounded. Then he settled down to wait and pray.

From his position on the hill, in the early light Will could make out the shapes of tipis and horses.

The quiet split with the boom of a cannon, shaking the ground, filling the air with smoke and the stench of gunpowder. Will shook himself to clear his head of images of Shiloh. He watched in fascinated horror as the cannon shells arced, whistled, and landed among the peaceful tipis. The camp bustled with war cries and screams. Each shell filled with canister shot pierced tipis and bodies with two hundred leaden balls at once. Will ducked, rolled on the ground, and covered his head. After a minute, he stood again.

Most of the Indians were on foot, unable to get to horses in time as the soldiers rode in among the tents, swinging sabers and firing pistols at point-blank range. The women ran screaming for the woods, holding on to their children, some clutching babies to their breasts. The Pawnee took no pity on them, shooting or bayoneting them as they ran. Soldiers concentrated on the warriors, but Will saw them firing on women as well in the confusion.

Where were the warriors? There were not many fighting men in the village. A group of about twenty fought their way to their horses and mounted, fleeing north with Conner and a squad of cavalry in pursuit. A few made it to the trees, turned, and began showering the soldiers with arrows.

Will was watching the battle, making sure the cavalry's horses didn't take flight. Concentrating, he jumped when he saw an Arapaho woman emerge from the trees, stumbling toward him in her headlong rush to get away. She had a young girl by the hand, running, tripping over rocks and roots. When she saw him, she froze, then drew a knife, pushing her daughter behind a log.

She stared at him, crouched, ready. Will, mindful of how dangerous he'd learned Dove could be, did not approach her. He moved sideways to the right, hoping for an opportunity to either disarm her or reassure her he meant no harm—not that she would believe him.

Will held up his hands so she could see he had no weapon in them. His Navy Colt stayed holstered at his side. For a long, tense moment, they stared at one another. Her face hardened with decision, and she barked a command at the hidden child, who jumped up and ran past her mother toward the eastern edge of the forest, away from the soldiers and the carnage of the village. When she was sure her child was safe, the mother turned and ran, melting into the forest.

When the battle wound down, the troops went through the village, looting, and burning. Occasional arrows still whizzed out of the woods, thumping into a log or a tree near the intended target, but the distance was too great to have much effect beyond fear and annoyance.

Six troopers were wounded, two killed. The ground was covered with Indian bodies in all manner of poses, lying where they'd fallen, some mothers on top of their children, protecting them as they'd both died. Conner permitted no aid to the Indian wounded. Troopers went through the village, shooting any warriors still living. They rounded up over one hundred women and children as prisoners. He ordered Gabe to interrogate a few of them. Most of the Arapaho men were absent on a raid of a Crow village, two days' ride away. Will saw Gabe and Conner arguing and swearing.

Conner looked over at him. "Crump! You seem to like these savages—see if you and Gabe can get the women to line up so I can talk to them."

Gabe scrunched his face into a scowl and motioned to Will. Coaxing and pointing, they got the women in a line. Conner mounted his horse. He looked at Frank North, head of the Pawnee scouts. "Frank, you interpret for me. You squaws—I want you to go to the reservation. Let them know that the United States Army is coming through this land. If you fight, we will kill you all, every last one."

He glared around at the group of women, slashing at his throat to make sure they understood.

"Go to the reservation. Keep the peace. Farm and raise your

families. I'm letting you go to carry the message."

Will looked around the camp, watching the burial detail, surveying the ruined tipis, the debris of battle. At one of the burned tipis, he saw scattered pots, an ax, and half-burned sleeping robes. He started to turn away when he heard a soft sound. Looking in that direction, he saw movement under a buffalo robe. When he pulled it back, dark eyes and a scrunched face broke into a full cry—a baby! Will picked up the child, bouncing it a little, hoping to quiet it. Walking over to where the soldiers guarded the women and children, he found a young woman with a toddler clutching her hand, pointed to the baby, and then to her. She seemed to understand and took the child. About an hour later, the order came to release the women and children due to Gabe's intervention. They trudged off into the snow, carrying their babies. They had no food.

Conner ordered the plunder and food from the village burned in a huge pyre, adding the bodies of the troopers killed to prevent the Arapaho mutilating the corpses.

Will cooked a light supper, fed the wounded soldiers, and got them ready for the march. It was after midnight when the troops, too weary to take another step, came struggling into the soldier camp.

"What now? Will the Indians chase us and attack?"

"Hard to say. They'll watch us for sure. Conner says rest here a day and then head for the rendezvous with the other troops."

"You mean back to Fort Laramie?"

"That direction anyways. To the Powder, then back."

Will's heart sank. "I don't suppose it would be safe for me to strike out on my own to Fort Bridger?"

Gabe chuckled. "Only if you like running from a nest of mad Arapaho."

"What if I wait a few days?"

"Wandering near four hundred miles, not knowing where you're going, with winter coming and Arapaho madder'n a grizzly in a trap, don't sound like good sense to me. But it's your hair."

Will's shoulders slumped. The thought of going back to where he'd started felt like rocks in his stomach. How would he ever find a place of peace?

Gabe looked at him and patted his shoulder. "Tell you what. I hear the soldiers will go out again in the spring. I owe Washakie a visit. Suppose I take you then? I've made the trip more'n a few times. Can't help you with the Sioux, the Blackfeet, or the Arapaho, but Washakie's band would give you a chance with me along. Maybe we could get that gal you brought in back to her people—if she hasn't taken off on her own."

Will looked up, hopeful. "That'd be great, Gabe."

The Pawnee went out again that night, serving as pickets to prevent the command from being taken unawares. Everyone but Gabe tried to sleep. Will tossed and turned, unable to get comfortable on the rocky ground, dreams haunting him. At first, he relived the horror of the day, screams and blood, bodies falling, whoops, and death. Then Will was back at Shiloh as Duke fell out of the saddle, or shooting at a legion of blue coats that never seemed to stop coming. Then he was back in prison, shivering and feverish. Just as dawn broke, he had managed to fall into a fitful but dreamless sleep. In minutes, he was jarred awake by the sound of reveille. By instinct, he was wide awake, grabbing his weapons, striking his tent, saddling Dusty.

With little but hardtack for breakfast, they broke camp and began the journey south, heading for the rendezvous with the other troops. Everyone was on edge. Tempers were short, and soon it appeared rations were even shorter. A suggestion from Will to go hunting was met with exasperation, Conner saying the soldiers had no time to look after a fool greenhorn.

Will stayed close to Gabe and began to see the folly of venturing out alone. The old scout pointed out tracks and signs. The Arapaho warriors must have returned from their raid and found their village destroyed. The troops were herding a large number of horses taken from the village. Gabe thought the warriors were shadowing them, looking for a chance to get their herd back.

Overnight, a cold front blew in. The wind was their constant unwelcome guest, by turns blowing sand or snow to sting their faces as they walked or rode. Forage was becoming difficult for the animals.

Mile after rugged mile, the troops moved south until one day they heard a great commotion ahead of them. North dispatched the Pawnee to scout. Two of them came back at a run, telling Conner there was a fight up ahead. Will whistled to Lightning to follow as he rode along with Gabe to see what the problem was. He put the cotton in his ears to avoid the sounds of battle.

Will and Gabe circled left, taking cover behind some rocks. Gabe could hear gunfire.

"Better bring that Spencer," he told Will, pointing at it. Will struggled to hear Gabe's voice through the cotton.

"They look surrounded," Will said.

"Yep. Judging from the slow firing, they're low on ammunition. Dang if it ain't Arapahoes too!"

"What should we do?"

"Wait for orders. But I 'spect Conner's gonna attack. We best be getting back."

They returned to their horses, mounted, and rode at a lope to the column. They reported to Conner and North.

Gabe spoke first, "Sir, we found a wagon train—could be your Nebraska volunteers you were planning to meet up with—under heavy attack. I'd judge near one hundred braves, Arapaho, circling the train."

Will said, "Sir, there's no women and children. Just warriors. I think the train is in a bad way. They could use our help, sir."

"Very well. Captain North, take Company F and the Pawnee and ride to the aid of the train. We have no rations or time for prisoners." Turning to Gabe and Will, he said, "Well, gentlemen?

Will you assist this time?"

Will surprised himself, almost not realizing he was speaking. "Yes, sir. I can see they are in need."

"Then try to set up crossfire. Take any ammunition you need from stores."

Will and Gabe returned to the rocks where they had observed the fight. Will went left, Gabe to the right. Gabe signaled, and each began to find targets. It wasn't long before the braves would not come to that side of the circled wagons. Then the Pawnee and the soldiers rode in, coming from two sides. Will and Gabe stopped firing to avoid hitting their men. Within a few minutes, the Arapaho gave up the fight, retreating to the west.

Will rode into the circle of wagons with Gabe. Conner joined them.

"Captain Sawyer at your service, sir! We were mighty glad to see you."

Gabe said nothing. Conner said, "We were glad to come to your aid. Have you had other encounters?"

"A few skirmishes, but nothing like this," said Sawyer.

Conner said, "We'll help you reach a fort not far from here. We're hoping to link up with the other parts of the expedition, see how they fared."

Will followed along behind the wagons, nervous and scanning the trees. He wished he had Gabe's sixth sense for trouble. Dusty seemed to catch Will's nervousness and danced along rather than just walking. Lightning whined and refused to go far from his side. For the fifth time, Will checked his revolver, making sure it was loaded, and the Spencer to make sure a cartridge was chambered. He'd told Conner that he'd served as rear guard for his unit in the war, but this was so different—an enemy that could not be seen or heard and didn't play by the usual rules.

As they saw Fort Conner, Will breathed a sigh of relief. Conner quickly mounted a guard and positioned the howitzers. They would be safe here for the moment.

Will settled in with the others to wait. Occasionally they saw deer or antelope within range of Will's or Gabe's rifle, and a foray would go out to collect the meat. Conner paced and kept going to the camp perimeter to stare at the prairie through his spyglass.

"Any signs, Gabe?" Conner asked.

Gabe spit a plug and returned sourly, "Signs of winter. Not much else. The game around here's gonna get scarce. You got figgered how you're gonna feed all these men, 'specially if the Arapaho come to surround this place?"

"Cole and Walker should be here soon. They'll bring provisions."

A week later, no troops had shown up. Conner's brow furrowed with worry.

"Gabe, I want you to take a few of the Pawnee and Captain North, scout farther north on the Powder, and see if you can find Cole and Walker. They should have been here by now. I'll wait two days, then start heading back. If we haven't heard from you or Cole by the time we reach the fort, I'll send a patrol after you."

"Sir, request that I accompany Gabe," said Will. "I'm not doing anyone any good here."

"Stay with Conner, greenhorn. Pawnee aren't always particular about who they scalp. Leshario here," said Gabe, pointing to a tall Pawnee, "is reliable. I'm leaving him to look out for you." Within hours, Gabe, North, and the Pawnee left.

Will was bone-weary from the constant vigilance. He couldn't decide which was worse, riding under constant threat of attack or sitting and waiting for something to happen. He volunteered for picket duty to alleviate the boredom.

All the next day, Will tried to stay out of sight and warm, with limited success. He lay next to Lightning, huddled into the dog's soft fur. Leshario came and went like a shadow that seemed unnervingly close but seldom seen.

As the sun set, Will thought of the freezing times in Camp Douglas during the war. He was just about to give in and ignore Gabe's warning about fires when he heard horses. Thinking it must be Gabe returning, he started to stand, then pulled back. Two braves were approaching on horseback, stopping now and then to look at the trail, as though tracking something.

They shouted, pointed at him, and charged, kicking their horses to a lope. The nearest one raised a war club, and Will's heart accelerated in fear. How could he take two of them? Lightning was running toward the horse—would he get trampled?

He drew the Colt without much time to aim, firing twice at the lead warrior from about twenty yards. Both shots hit mid-chest, and the warrior hesitated but urged the horse to bear down on Will, the war club raised to strike. The club struck his shoulder a glancing blow on the arm not holding the gun. Will dropped and rolled to the right, coming up on one knee, and fired twice more: once at the warrior, once at the horse. This time his enemy toppled off the horse and lay still. Turning, Will saw Leshario grappling with the other warrior, a knife inches from his throat. He ran over, put one shot in the enemy, and then clubbed him over the head with the butt of the empty pistol. Then Will collapsed. When he woke, Lightning was licking his face.

Will's arm was throbbing. Leshario stood over him. They looked at each other, chests heaving. Leshario extended a hand and helped Will up. They took the weapons from their adversaries. Will had to reload to put the pony he'd shot out of its misery. The other stood a short distance away, eyes white and bulging. A paint, it looked like a good mount, and Will was happy to let Leshario have it.

Men began running over, rifles at the ready after hearing the shots. Conner came last. When he saw the dead warriors, he smiled.

"Looks like Johnny Reb's worth something after all. Corporal, post extra guards. There's bound to be more of them."

Will hoped Gabe would return soon. He flexed his arm—no bones seemed broken. He stumbled to the medic tent to have his shoulder bandaged. He knew they were perhaps five to seven days away from Fort Conner, and he'd no idea how far ahead Gabe and the other Pawnee had gone. He felt alone, confused, and afraid. Peace? What a joke! He'd wandered into a war.

Night fell, but Gabe did not come. Will prayed, looked at the stars, and wondered if some misfortune had befallen the wily old mountain man.

Will could find no rest. Leshario stood watch over Will and the horses. Will tried to sleep but woke with a start each time he dozed, plagued by dreams of the war and thoughts of Sioux creeping up on them.

When dawn came, Will decided Bridger had fallen. He thought of trying to go north, see if he and Leshario could catch Gabe's trail, maybe somehow effect a rescue. After prayer and thought, he rejected the idea. If Gabe couldn't make it back, wouldn't it be folly to think he could get through?

Will was contemplating going to Conner when he heard them . . . horses. Lots of them . . . and men. He panicked—what if the Sioux had come? What if this Pawnee was selling them out? He remembered what Gabe had said: the Sioux took no adult male prisoners.

An Indian came through the trees, and Will aimed. But

Leshario slapped the gun, and the shot went wild. Will was furious and turned the gun on Leshario when he saw Gabe coming through the trees behind the Indian, who was another Pawnee scout.

"What, ho there, greenhorn! Trying to take on the whole Sioux nation?"

Will felt foolish. He holstered his gun. Now he could see a line of blue-clad troops following Gabe—they must be Cole's men. As he looked closer, he saw many of the uniforms were in rags and the men were barefoot, with bloody, torn feet. They looked like scarecrows stumbling along, as though they hadn't eaten in a fortnight. A few officers had horses, but most were on foot. Leshario called out a greeting to his fellow Pawnee.

Gabe came over. "Gave me up for dead, didn't cha? Well, can't blame you none. Coulda been the truth. Sioux bothered us all the way back. 'Spect they'll keep it up. Wish we could rest the men; they've had a hard march and little food. Why don't you take Leshario and see if you can find a deer or two? Don't go farther than he says, though—he saved your hair once today already."

Within two hours, Will and Leshario came back with two fat bucks, which were skinned and roasted, food for Cole's hungry troops. They set out on their two hundred-mile march south, back to Fort Conner.

There were a few skirmishes on the way back. Will could not see where the arrows came from, but he fired a few rounds to discourage them. When they arrived at Fort Conner, everyone was hungry and exhausted. Some of the men had nothing but rags left to cover their bleeding feet.

Will spent time with the wounded. It was an opportunity to learn more practical medicine from Gabe.

"How did you get away?" Will asked a soldier.

"We had the range on 'em. My Spencer can shoot farther than their arrows, but the barrel got so hot I couldn't hold it. Then we'd gallop a ways. Tough on my leg and my friend, but we kept going." He grimaced as Gabe tugged on the arrow shaft in his right leg.

"Take some whiskey; we'll come back in a bit. This is gonna hurt. But I think we can save the leg."

The supply wagons were empty except for the seriously wounded. They made it back to Fort Laramie, hampered by a lack of rations and forage for the animals.

The Powder River Expedition ended on a whimper. Will was no closer to his goal of a peaceful place to live as winter began.

CHAPTER SEVEN

Dove paced in her cell. She could flex her arm and pick up light objects with it now. The food the soldiers gave her wasn't great, but it kept her alive.

She peered out her barred window—something was happening. Soldiers were running to and fro and saddling horses as the whole fort pulsed with energy. She heard shouts—could it be? Was the expedition returning? Maybe Gabe could help her. She heard bugles and soldiers.

She strained to see out as the soldiers came through the gate in a column of twos. Gabe was easy to recognize with his slouch brimmed hat and relaxed manner.

She was surprised to see Will and Dusty come at a gallop, bringing up the rear behind the soldiers. Will hadn't left the others after all.

She poked at the stove in the corner, trying to coax some flame from the meager embers. They didn't often give her wood, just enough to keep from freezing. She had no warm buffalo robe, as she might have at home. Home! There was a word that brought longing to her heart. How she wished to be back with her people, away from this strange white man's world.

She sat on the rude log bench, closed her eyes, and escaped in her mind. She was on a pony, flying over the prairie, feeling the wind ruffle her hair, the sun warm on her face. She could almost feel the motion of the pony, the pounding hooves . . .

Her reverie was interrupted—someone was pounding on her door, not just in her dream. She frowned, returning to the present, and walked to the door. She looked through the window and saw Will.

"Dove, are you well? I just found out about you being in here. They won't let me take you out. There's to be a trial, a time for truth. I'll do everything I can to make sure the truth comes out."

She shook her head and smiled sadly. "They'll never believe me. It's the word of an Indian squaw against a white man."

"We have to make them believe. I just heard Conner isn't in charge anymore. Maybe the new commander . . ."

"I just want to go home."

"I promise . . . I'll do my best to see that you make it home."

Will stuck a hand through the bars, and she clasped it. She didn't dare to hope, but she knew he wanted to help.

The next day, Will began asking questions to anyone who would talk to him. The new commander forced the returning troops to camp outside the fort. Most had been ruled unfit for service and would march back toward Leavenworth and muster out when the weather allowed, leaving one hundred active troops to protect the fort and hundreds of square miles of territory.

Will went to Clarissa.

"Clarissa, did you see anything the day the fight happened? Anything at all?"

"Well, no. I wasn't there. But all the women know about Buckman. He isn't to be trusted."

"Would any women testify about him bothering them in the past?"

"Probably not. It might affect their husbands' careers, and no woman would want others to think she . . . invited the situation. It would damage her reputation. Sorry to say, most of the wives would think it's not worth it for the sake of a squaw, an Indian. What will happen to her?"

"If the commander doesn't believe her, she'll hang."

Clarissa looked shocked. "I'll talk to some of the other women—and my father. I'll see what I can do."

"Can you show me where it happened?"

"Sure, at least what Dove told me."

They walked over to the horse corral. Lightning followed, sniffing the ground. Will looked around.

"It's pretty far away from the rest of the buildings. Did Dove say why she was over this far?"

"No. Everyone thinks she was trying to steal a horse."

Will looked at the horses in the corral and pointed out a pony.

"Isn't that the one she rode? Sure looks like it to me. Except now it's got a US brand on it. Seems to me she wasn't the one stealing a horse."

Clarissa's brow furrowed. "I see what you mean. You think maybe she was thinking of leaving with her horse?"

"Seems the most logical explanation. Then Buckman comes along, starts bothering her, she's scared, fights back. Most any woman would."

"But not many white women carry skinning knives on them," Clarissa pointed out. "Couldn't do much damage."

"If everyone knows about Buckman, why don't the officers do something about him?"

"You've been in the army. You should know when a post is shorthanded, you don't go looking for reasons to get rid of a soldier."

Will admitted it was true.

"Well, keep thinking. We have maybe a month to come up with something. Carrington has to get settled into his command, learn the facts. They're sending a judge advocate, I heard—Washington got so much backlash over the Dakota hangings, they want it done right."

Walking back to his tent outside the fort, Will saw a group of women gathered, talking. They pointed at him, then the guardhouse by the river. He could see the frowns; he didn't need to hear the conversation to know it was disapproving gossip.

Will visited Dove daily, sometimes with Gabe when he wasn't out scouting. Each time Will came by, she seemed to soften a little more. Smiling, she asked about his arm and extended friendship. She seemed to understand that he was trying to help and encourage her.

Dove couldn't add much to what they already knew about the incident. The problem was going to be getting people to believe her. She admitted she'd been thinking of taking the horse. Will had heard about the hanging of Dakota Indians a few years back for defending their homeland against the depredations of white settlers. Lincoln's intervention had prevented even more deaths. He was thankful Conner was gone and wouldn't be presiding—Will heard he'd hanged Indians on the scantest evidence in the past.

The day of the trial arrived. Dove expected no mercy. She'd seen the white man's mercy at Bear River. As far as she knew, no one had found anything to help her. The weather was cloudy, freezing, and threatening snow or sleet. It suited her mood. She could expect no rescue. Gabe had left, gone back east. Clarissa and Will were the only friendly faces here. Clarissa had come less of late due to her father's influence.

She was frightened but resolved. If it was her time to make the journey to the Great Spirit, then so be it. She would not cry or wail or give the white man any satisfaction. She would make her mother proud, like a true Shoshone. If the chance to escape presented itself, she would take it.

Two soldiers came to the door of the cell and opened it.

"Get out here, squaw!" said the burly sergeant. "It's time for justice."

She stared at them defiantly, pretending not to understand. The other soldier, a private, came into the cell and reached for her arm. She stood and shook him off. He jumped back as though afraid she might magically produce the knife they'd taken from her and cut him. The sergeant laughed.

"Afraid of this little wildcat, O'Malley? Nothing to worry about. She's going to dance at the end of a rope."

Dove stiffened her spine, held her head up, and walked between them. The private was no more than a boy. In her tribe, he might be joining his first war party to hold the horses. Here, he was supposed to be a full-fledged warrior but was afraid of a woman. Looking to her right, she gauged the distance to the river—if she dropped and rolled, could she run to the river before they shot her? She doubted it.

The infantry mess hall was now a makeshift courtroom. General Carrington and Major O'Brien presided. O'Brien took the lead since Carrington had just arrived. Dove was seated at a front table on a bench beside a young man with hair on both sides of his face who looked younger than her brother of five and twenty summers.

"All rise! This court will come to order, the United States versus the Shoshone woman known as Dove. All who have matters before this court draw near and be heard."

Turning to Dove, the man said, "Since you are the accused and indigent, the court has appointed counsel for you. You may refuse that counsel, but it would be inadvisable. Do you accept or refuse?"

Dove looked at the man, confused. Her mind whirled. Fear gripped her, and she tried to comprehend. If only Gabe were here . . .

"Do you understand?"

She shook her head, the white man's signal for no. In her fear and confusion, English fled her mind. A flood of Shoshone words wanted to come, but she knew they would not understand. She might as well be dead before it started.

O'Brien and the others looked puzzled, unsure what to do with her. Then O'Brien motioned to one of the guards, whispered in his ear, and the guard left, returning minutes later with one of the Pawnee that stayed around the post, Tokala.

"Tokala, I know you speak English, from missionary school. Can you also understand this woman?"

Tokala turned to her and spoke in Shoshone, "The white chief wants me to speak his words to you and yours to him. What shall I say?"

"Tell him . . . tell him I want to go home. I am peaceful. I've done nothing. Tell him I want my horse."

Tokala translated. O'Brien looked satisfied, though irritated at her cheek in asking for the horse.

"All right, that's solved. Adjutant, proceed."

"Prosecution, call the first witness."

"Private Buckman!"

Buckman came forward, swore his oath on the Bible, and leered in Dove's direction.

Dove tensed at the sight of her attacker. Her mouth felt dry, and she clenched her fists.

"Private Buckman, do you recognize this woman?"

Tokala began to whisper translation, but Dove waved him off, her forehead creased in concentration. She must hear all the words, understand the English. She must.

"Yes, sir. That is to say, sort of. All of them Indians look a lot alike."

"What happened on the day in question?"

"I was coming off guard duty, went over to the sutler's to pay my back bill. Saw this woman standing outside the corrals down the road apiece. Warn't no reason for an Injun being over there. I walked over to see what she was doing. She was bending over to slip through the rails, had a halter. I thought she was trying to steal a horse—Lord knows the Injuns stole enough of our herd already. I grabbed her to try and stop her. Quick as a snake, she turned and slashed me with a knife. Sawbones had to sew me up once he got sober."

Dove jumped to her feet. "You lie! I had no halter."

The judge banged his gavel. "Order! Counsel, restrain your client, or she will be removed."

Buckman smirked and rolled up his sleeve to display a long, jagged scar.

"Lucky she didn't hit nothing mortal. Well, I fought back o' course, and she fainted. So did I. Woke up in my bunk, thankful I still had my scalp."

"I see. But hadn't the woman been injured? Was she often about the post grounds?"

"Don't rightly know about that. I s'pose I heard a hurt Injun was brought in with Old Gabe. Can't recall I ever seen her much."

"Did you do anything besides grab her arm? Something she might have thought was threatening to make her attack you?"

"Why, 'course not. Why would I bother with an Injun? I just thought she was stealing a horse."

Dove's mouth set in a tight line, her fists clenched.

"Thank you, Private Buckman. No further questions."

O'Brien turned to the young lieutenant at Dove's side. "Any questions from the defense?"

"Not at this time, sir."

"Any further witnesses?"

"No, sir. I think Private Buckman was pretty clear on what happened. No one else around. We got the word of a soldier against an Indian."

Dove's shoulders slumped, and the fight went out of her when Tokala translated. It was as she feared. There was no hope. Certainly not from any of the white men supposedly defending her. If only they would let her fight—she would die trying. But that was not the white man's way. They would threaten to shoot her, then tie a rope around her neck. She would have to sing a death song before she got there. She looked around, hoping to catch a glimpse of Will. Had he abandoned her? Clarissa, of course, would not be allowed to come to the trial.

The lieutenant was standing up now. Dove thought he would betray her.

"If it pleases the court, we do have witnesses for the defense."

O'Brien looked startled. Clearly, he'd thought the whole trial a formality.

"What witnesses? The squaw? You're not serious."

"No, sir, other witnesses. We call Will Crump."

"Very well, though I don't see what the secesh has to do with this matter."

Just then, Will walked into the courtroom with a little boy of about eight years old in tow. Entrusting the boy to a soldier, he strode to the front of the court, took the oath, and was seated.

"Mr. Crump, did you enter the post with this woman a few months back?"

"Yes, sir. She helped save me from some Cheyenne and got wounded in the process. I tried to help her by bringing her here."

"And when you brought her to the post, did she have a horse?"

"Yes, sir, an Indian pony."

"And where is that horse now?"

"In the post corral, sir."

The lieutenant affected surprise.

"So she entered the post with a pony, and that pony is in the corral."

"Yes, sir. Now it's branded US like you Yankees own it."

"The defendant, then, was merely trying to reclaim her horse."

"That's the way I see it. I wasn't there, but that's her horse right enough."

"No further questions."

O'Brien turned to the prosecutor.

"And you, sir?"

"With pleasure. Mr. Crump, were you ever in the Army of the United States?"

"No, sir."

"So you claim you never broke your oath, that you are truthful and trustworthy, even though you took up arms against your country?”

Will's look would have melted iron. Dove saw his determination.

“Sir, I took an oath to John Hunt Morgan and the Lexington Rifles. I stuck to that oath, though it led me to capture, prison, and near death. I defended my home state from the invading Yankee army and obeyed my officers, as I'm sure you obeyed yours. The war is over. I did not, even in the prison camp, renounce my oath. But John Morgan and the Confederacy have fallen, and that oath is dead. You may check my records, if they exist in Richmond.”

“Very admirable, I'm sure. But we have only your word for it, just as we only have your word that this squaw had a horse, the one in the corral. Are there not a great many such horses? Could you not be mistaken?”

“Sir, I was in the cavalry during the war. I learned a great deal about horses. The one she rode had a white sock on the right rear leg, and a front hoof turned in and up. Some might say it is unsound, but I believe it gives the beast speed. It was true of a Morgan I rode, and there wasn't another horse like it.”

“But of course, you have an attachment to this woman. Perhaps she became your squaw? Wouldn't you say anything to save her?”

Will looked over at Dove and hesitated. “No, sir. I would not. Honor is very precious to me.”

“Well, my honorable young secesh, you expect us to believe that after months in the field and time here back at the fort, you will so well remember a horse that was of little consequence to you?”

The defense rose to object.

“All right, all right. I'll withdraw that. No further questions.”

Will stepped down from the stand and went to the young lieutenant, whispering in his ear and pointing to the dirty boy in the back.

O'Brien began to lose patience.

"Do you have anything further, Lieutenant?"

"Yes, sir. I want to call Luke O'Leary."

O'Brien again looked surprised. "I hope this is relevant and not just a further waste of our time."

"I assure you, sir, I have this witness, and one more, Miss Clarissa Cochran. If someone would be so good as to bring her round, we will take as little of the court's time as possible."

"Sergeant! Have someone fetch Miss Cochran. Proceed, sir."

"Luke, do you understand about telling the truth?"

"Yes, sir. It's very bad to lie. My pa taught me that 'fore he died."

"And do you promise on the Holy Bible and all the saints to tell the truth here?"

"Yes, sir."

"Very well. Do you remember this man?" The Lieutenant pointed at Buckman.

"Yes, sir. I remember him all right. He thrashed me once for not having his horse ready fast enough."

"Do you work in the stable? Around the corrals?"

"Yes, sir. Ever since Indians killed my pa and my ma died with the fever. It's how I make my bread."

"And what about her?" said the lieutenant, pointing at Dove.

"I remember her right enough. Took her horse when she came in. I heard lots of talk about her, but she seemed all right to me."

"You don't hate her because of what happened to your father?"

"No, sir. My pa and the priest taught me the Good Book. The priest, he used to tell me about love your enemies if you wanna go to heaven. And Jesus, he forgave the guys that nailed him to the cross."

"Anything else you remember about her?"

"Yes, sir. There come a day, I was in the barn, cleaning harness. Looked out and saw her by the corral. I hadn't seen her out walking before—maybe she was too hurt. Anyhow, I was curious. So I watched her a bit. She seemed to be looking at the horse she came in on. She walked a little closer to the fence, then Mr. Buckman showed up, started talking to her. Couldn't hear altogether what was said, but she didn't seem to like it none. She moved away, and he grabbed her like he was gonna do sumpin' to her. She pulled her knife and cut him. He let go, staggered a little, and fainted. She stood breathing for a minute, and then she passed out."

"And you could see all of this?"

"Yes, sir."

"And did you report it, get help for them, Luke?"

Luke lowered his head, shamefaced. "No, sir. I didn't want no trouble."

"So why are you talking now? Are you getting back at Private Buckman for thrashing you?"

"No, sir. The secesh there, he was asking around about what happened. I heard she might get hung over it. Injun or not, don't think nobody should get hung for sumpin' they didn't do. He was picking on a woman. Got no call to do that. Reckon if I had a sister, and she had a knife, she'd a done the same."

"No further questions."

"Prosecution?"

"No questions, sir."

"I call Clarissa Cochran."

Clarissa came forward, and the clerk swore her in.

"Miss Cochran, would you agree that you have been friends with the defendant?"

"Yes, sir. She was hurt, and she seemed alone and lost."

"Are you familiar with Private Buckman?"

Clarissa looked angry. "Yes, sir. I believe you'd find most of the women on the post are familiar with Mister Buckman."

"How so?"

"He harasses any pretty girl he can find."

"You mean he tries to . . . take familiarities?"

"Yes, sir. I experienced it once, at the Christmas party last year."

"And did you report it?"

"No, sir. He was drunk. I wasn't hurt. I didn't want anyone to think I'd encouraged him, so I let it go."

"And you're speaking up now to help your friend?"

"Yes, sir."

"Your witness."

The prosecutor rose. "Miss Cochran, we all respect loyalty— even to a squaw. But isn't it just a little too convenient that you are speaking up now? Why not before? I assume you don't have a reputation of . . . encouraging men in the wrong way?"

"I'm no trollop, sir!" said Clarissa. "If you don't believe me, you can ask the major's wife!"

Shock rippled through the courtroom. Dove saw it on O'Brien's face, followed by anger.

O'Brien spoke in terse, clipped words. "Miss Cochran, explain yourself. And think well—your father's career may rest on it."

"Major, I know she wouldn't want you to know, but I can't keep quiet while that . . . that man causes Dove to get hung for something he did to so many women here. After that Christmas party, when I ran away from him, I came back, thinking maybe I'd tell my pa. I came in behind your house after I'd been up the hill to think a bit. I saw him—he had your wife by both arms like he was trying to . . . to . . . kiss her! I made noise, threw a rock against the house, and hid. He let her go, and she ran inside. I waited and went around the front. When I talked to her later, she begged me not to tell, afraid you'd be angry or think she did something to bring it on."

"Sergeant! Will you fetch my wife, please? Let's get to the bottom of this."

A few minutes later, Caitlin O'Brien walked in, nervous and tearful. Dove could see great confusion on her face.

Tokala bent and whispered in Shoshone, "White chief's woman. Very scared, I think."

Major O'Brien dispensed with formalities. "Mrs. O'Brien,

this girl says that Private Buckman attempted to be . . . familiar with you at the party last Christmas. Is this true?"

Caitlin looked down and stammered, "Yes, but . . . please don't think badly of me. I . . . just left the party for a few minutes. I . . . had to use the privy. When I came back, Private Buckman engaged me in conversation. I didn't wish to be rude, so I stopped to talk for a moment. He . . . he . . . grabbed me, and I resisted. There was a noise—it startled him, made him afraid, I think. I broke free and ran back into the house. Please, John! Don't be angry with me!"

O'Brien stood. "Indeed not! Gentlemen, do we need further proof? This woman is innocent. Release her. Sergeant! Arrest Private Buckman! This court is adjourned."

CHAPTER EIGHT

The winter dragged on, with Dove on edge, nervous about revenge from white soldiers after Buckman's humiliation and worried at being surrounded by Crows, who had come in for the winter. Spotted Tail's Sioux wintered elsewhere, a great blessing to her. Buckman, at least, was gone—arrested and sent to Leavenworth for a general court-martial. After he left, more stories of abuse came out. All the women of the post breathed a sigh of relief at his removal.

Carrington, the new commander, wanted no more trouble. He ordered Dove outside the fort, across the bridge over the Platte. No Indians allowed in the post without permission. She set up her lodge as close to the bridge as possible for fear of the Crows.

Dove wanted to find some way to thank Will for his help at the trial. She couldn't think of anything yet but found he occupied her thoughts often. For now, she settled for treating him with friendship and respect.

Will helped her pass the time, Clarissa visited, and her English progressed. There was little else to do besides making moccasins, tanning hides, drying, and cooking venison that Will brought in from hunting. She could see he was restless.

O'Brien returned her horse to her, an unusual kind gesture considering that the post was short on mounts for the soldiers. She didn't dare ride far from the fort, with the weather and the Crow about, but at least occasionally she and Will could break free from the fort routine and escape into the country when the snow was not too deep and the temperature above zero.

The winter was severe, and Dove was glad not to be in the guardhouse with no wood. They kept a fire going most of the time and sheltered from the wind under elk and buffalo robes. Will had a little money left and traded with the Crow for two new buffalo hides, which Dove prepared. It promised to be a long winter.

She watched as Will cleaned his Spencer. Lightning lay curled at his feet. In the weeks since the trial, they had said little about it. He seemed to expect nothing of her, assuming the role of provider and protector. Why? Why was he doing this? A few teased him about her being his squaw, but he either ignored them or refuted it. Any debt he might have felt from the incident with the Cheyenne was more than repaid by his bringing her to the fort and proving her innocence at the trial.

"What will you do now?" she asked him.

Will looked up and smiled as he rammed the cleaning cloth down the barrel.

"I promised to get you home. That's what I intend to do. Soon as the weather lets up, we can head out."

"You don't know what you're saying. It's many sleeps to the place of my people. You've never been there. You don't know where to go. The Sioux and Arapaho are everywhere now."

"Better than you going on your own."

"I know how to hunt. I know how to move unseen. My brother Wolf will help me. Why would you risk yourself for me?"

Will looked down, fiddling with the fringe on his jacket, his face turning red.

"Well, where I come from, women are supposed to be protected. Especially a woman you care about."

He looked at her thoughtfully.

"I guess I have a sister a bit like you—Albinia's her name. She goes ahead and does whatever she thinks is right, without much thought for what might happen. She did a lot of things during the war and before that, if my pa had known, he wouldn't have let her. I . . . I should have spoken up, but I didn't. Guess I'm trying to make up for it. Besides," he grinned, "I can be awful stubborn when I make a promise." He looked more serious. "I do care what happens to you. Most folks would think I'm crazy, caring about an Indian, man or woman. But I do care, and there it is. I think God wants me to make sure you make it home, so you're gonna have a hard time talking me out of it.”

Dove stared at the fire and continued working on the moccasins she'd started. Did she dare ask anything more?

“Why are you here, Will Crump? Why come all this way if you have a family you care about?”

“Searching, I guess. Maybe I'm different than you and your people. In the war, I followed someone I admired. I thought I'd have a better life. But it just led to killing. Then I was put in prison . . . You know what that's like. I still have nightmares, feel guilt for the men I killed and the ones I couldn't save. I thought maybe if I could find a little land in the woods, build a cabin of my own, I could live in peace. It seemed like all I heard about was people going west. My family had a place for me, but I . . . I relive the war. Gunshots sometimes send me back to it. Once I even pointed a pistol at my little sister because she woke me in the middle of a dream about the war. I thought up in the mountains, I could find peace. The war took almost everything— my family's farm, the girl I cared for, many friends. I even found myself wondering about God; both sides in the war claimed that God was on their side. How could God let there be so much suffering, so much killing? Isn't there any place where a fella can live in peace, nobody wanting anything from him, no worries about what color someone's skin is? If I could find a place like that, and then maybe someone to share it with, I could heal. Maybe then I'd be ready for being normal, whatever that is. Think I'm crazy?”

“No. Your dream is not so different from mine or my people's. We want to live as we always have, ever since the horses came. But the *Bagiwiga* and the *Pampittsimminna*—how do you call? The Blackfeet, the Sioux, the Cheyenne, they take our hunting grounds, capture women, give us no peace. Then the army, men like Connor, come. They kill us for no reason. They lie, they cheat, they steal. Soldiers kill women and children. Whites call us savages. We feel no guilt about the death of an enemy. But that does not make us any more savage than your soldiers.”

Visions from the massacre at Bear River filled her mind.

Dispelling them, she changed the subject. "This woman you lost in your war, what happened to her?"

A flash of pain crossed Will's face. "I don't know. I had a chance to visit home—the war was all around us. Her mother said the enemy came and abused her. She . . . she wasn't in her right mind after that. She left. I don't know where she went."

"Will you go and find her?"

"No. That's over. Even if I did, she's either crazy or has found someone else by now. It's best to let it go."

"Do you love her still?"

"I don't know, to be honest. We were so young . . . It seems a lifetime ago. I don't know if love was ever there. But it doesn't matter now. What about you? Is someone waiting for you?"

"With my people, a woman has little choice in marriage. It's up to her father. Before the Cheyenne took me, my father considered joining me with a man from our band, Kajika. He is a great warrior, a good hunter and provider. But . . ."

"But you don't care for him?"

"It isn't for me to say. Father had misgivings about him. He has a mean streak and isn't one to think of others. I think my father worries about how he would treat me."

The fire was burning low, and the sun began to set. Dove rose, got wood from the nearby pile, and set about roasting some venison from the day before. They lapsed into a thoughtful silence.

The bugle blew, signaling riders approaching the fort. March was beginning, and it wasn't always freezing at night. People were starting to travel on the plains. A second alarm went up, and everyone rushed to saddle horses. A large party of Sioux was approaching.

Will saw that Dove was very uneasy at the approaching party. He went to Major O'Brien.

"Sir, a small matter. The Sioux and Shoshone are enemies. Dove is fearful of being outside the fort with none of her people here. The Crow will not protect her. Might she come in the fort, at least while the Sioux are here?"

"If you'll stay with her and take responsibility for her. Can't have another incident like Buckman. And now I'm very busy. I have to see what these Sioux want. We're not in good shape for a battle, if that's what they've come for."

"Yes, sir. Thank you, sir."

Will and Dove went to the sutlers.

"Hey, you can't bring her in here!" the sutler objected. His wife spoke, "Now, Henry . . . the poor girl is just trying to get warm."

"We just want to sit by the stove and stay away from the Sioux."

"Sioux? Where?"

"Large party coming in from the west. Wish Gabe were here to parley with them. Is it all right? Can we sit by your fire if we buy a few things?"

Hearing the prospect of money, the sutler grumbled a little and acquiesced. Dove and Will settled on a bench near the fire. The sutler kept glancing over like he wanted to make sure Dove wasn't stealing anything. Will bought a few peppermints and deciding to splurge on some coffee. This seemed to satisfy the storekeeper.

After an hour or so, they were surprised to see Clarissa come in. They had seen less of her, living outside the gates of the fort.

"I wondered if I might find you here. Spotted Tail, the Sioux leader, has come in. Not for war, but for peace! Father doesn't trust them, but it sounds very positive. There's talk of a big peace conference, maybe a new treaty in a few months. He brought his daughter who died this winter. She requested burial here, and it sounds like O'Brien will let them. Spotted Tail speaks good English. I was surprised. He says no more war."

"That is good news," said Will. Looking over at Dove, he said, "Do you think it might be safe to move to your people?"

"No. I would not trust Spotted Tail. Besides, the snows still may come. The game will be scarce. It would be better to wait. In one or two moons, my people will move to summer ranges."

Clarissa frowned. "Are you still talking about leaving? I'd hoped maybe you'd settle somewhere near here. With all the trouble going on, it would be safer near the fort."

Will smiled. "Thanks, but Dove wants to go home, and I want to see she gets there. We'll head out when the weather breaks."

Dove had been right—more snows came. Most days, she hunkered down with Will, tried to stay out of the wind, and talked of past times. At last, the weather seemed to warm, the skies to clear, and whispers of spring spoke to them. There had been no word of Gabe, so as April waned and May began, they agreed to set out.

"Should we start laying in stores for travel?" Will asked her. "It can't hurt to be ready."

"Yes, we don't know when the weather will break. We need medicine, herbs, bandages, and ammunition. I can hardly believe we're going to my home! My father and mother will be so surprised to see me!"

She surprised Will by trading some furs he'd brought in over the winter for a mule to carry extra supplies.

"You lead. You know the country, I don't. I wish Gabe were here to go with us, but no one knows when or if he'll be back, so that leaves just us."

"It's a risk. With Spotted Tail vowing peace, perhaps we will make it. I have to try. I have nowhere else to go."

They started in the gray light of dawn to avoid attracting attention. Dove led them southwest, saying that there was a mountain range to go around and fewer Sioux to the south, but plenty of Cheyenne. They forded the Platte near Deer Creek. Will trailed Dove and the mule carrying the tent, food, and medical supplies. He didn't know whether to believe the stories some of the soldiers told, but by most accounts, if they encountered hostile Indians, it would be a fight to the death.

The wind began to pick up, and Will wrapped his muffler tighter around his face. He marveled at how Dove seemed immune to the cold because she was so excited to be on the home trek. They arrived at another crossing for the Platte, and the mule balked. Lightning swam back and forth, trying to encourage the mule, it seemed. But it was no use. Rather than fight him, making noise and wasting time, they decided to follow the river west in its undulating, looping trajectory until a better crossing.

An hour later, following a game trail, they found a sandbar projecting into the river, making the crossing much narrower. The water had not yet gotten the snowmelt from the mountains, and it looked as though it might not be over two feet deep at that point. If the mule refused to cross here, they'd have to keep following the river, taking them miles out of the way.

Dove stopped and motioned him forward.

"This is the best crossing we'll find for miles," she said. "But look at the sandbar . . . What do you see?"

"Looks like a lot of horses passed here, and not that long ago."

"Right. We are too far from the fort for any help from there. We need to go carefully. Make as little noise as possible. No fire tonight. I hope it is not *de'ase*—what's the word?"

"Freezing," Will supplied.

He was making an effort to learn her language as well.

Dove crossed on her pony. The lead rope was long enough for her horse to make it onto the far bank while the mule was still on the sandbar. She looked backward at the mule, who was digging its hind legs in against the pull of the rope.

Will sighed. "All right, let me try something. He tied Dusty to a low bush, rummaged through his saddlebag, and came up with one of the peppermint sticks from the sutler.

He walked around to the front of the mule and broke off a small piece. He let the mule sniff it, lick it, then gobble it. Then he held a piece just out of reach so that the mule had to walk forward a step or two to get it. Will moved back, stepping into the river. His feet would be wet and cold, but he could dry out later. One thing was sure—they couldn't stay here all night. Will was beginning to think the mule was more trouble than he was worth.

The mule took a tentative step, then two. It stopped when its front feet hit the water, so Will brought the peppermint stick closer, then farther away. "Come on, boy. If I can stand the cold water, you can. Just a little farther."

Will was absorbed in getting the mule across, having reached about halfway. Will's boots had just reached solid ground on the bank when an arrow came from Dove's side of the river and hit the saddlebag on the mule with a *thwock.*

The mule spooked, rearing and pulling hard on the lead rope. He bucked and pulled Dove off her pony. She landed in the brush. Everything happened at once—war whoops, arrows filling the air, the mule out of control, spilling their supplies into the river. Will put the mule between him and the arrows, drawing his pistol. He looked toward Dove and saw two Indians moving toward her through the brush. If only he had his rifle! He fired and saw one of the Indians fall. The mule bucked again, blocking his next shot. Abandoning the mule, he lunged back toward Dusty. An arrow caught the mule in the throat and another pierced Will's boot.

Ignoring the wound, he untied Dusty and mounted. Now he could fight back! He pulled the Spencer from the scabbard and aimed as two braves came across the stream toward him. Lightning barked, growled, and charged, hitting the one fitting an arrow on his bowstring. Will fired, and they moved no more. He felt a piercing pain in his head, and his vision swam for a moment. When it cleared, his attention shifted back across the stream. Where was Dove?

The mule had taken a few steps toward the bank and fallen. Will kicked Dusty forward on the sandbank using the quarter horse's instant speed to sail over the fallen mule. Will saw a few Indian ponies kicking up dust ahead in the distance.

Dove was gone.

Slung across a horse facedown, hands tied behind her back with a thong, there was little Dove could do but hope she didn't fall off and get crushed under pounding hooves. Then again, maybe that would be better considering what awaited her at the hands of these three Sioux warriors. Her arms ached, her ribs were sore, and every jounce of the horse threatened to knock her wind out. After a few minutes, the ponies slowed to a walk. She supposed that meant there was no pursuit. Will must be dead or wounded. There would be no rescue.

After an hour of walking, the ponies stopped. The warrior that held her captive yanked her off the horse so that she fell, striking her head. She rolled, and he kicked her hard in the stomach, laughing. She spat at him and got a fist in the side of her face. After that, she lay still, wondering if a knife or rape was next. There was little she could do about either. She was beginning to feel numb in her hands. She risked moving her head to see better. The warriors had wandered off a short distance, seeming to ignore her for the moment. They didn't seem to think she would crawl away—and they were right, at least for now.

Her head hurt, her ribs felt broken, and she was thirsty. Almost every part of her was in misery, but she knew it could get worse, much worse. If she pretended to be more injured, perhaps after dark they would let down their guard, enabling escape. They might not hunt her down. They had her pony, and maybe a squaw wasn't worth the trouble.

Her captor returned and, using another thong, tied her legs together at the ankles. At least he's not planning rape, she thought. But how could she escape bound hand and foot? The captor's hands got exploratory, moving up her thigh. She felt sick and tried to squirm away. He laughed, calling her something like a snake or a worm. He moved away and returned in a few minutes with his pony. He slung her over the pony again, this time tying her hands to her feet underneath the pony. Satisfied she wasn't going anywhere, he mounted the pony, and the group moved out again at a slow trot. Each bounce was agony, shooting pain through her ribs and abdomen.

They traveled for another hour, the sun beginning to sink behind the western horizon and the temperature dropping. They went down into a draw, surrounded on three sides by rock, and made camp. One of the other braves went back over their trail, wiping it out with a sagebrush branch. They risked a fire but didn't worry too much about getting her close enough to it for comfort. Her captor squatted down beside her, taking out his knife.

Was this it? She looked wildly around for a rock or something she could grab. He laughed again at her fear. He grabbed her face between both hands, twisting her neck, forcing her to look at him. He signed slitting her throat and then pointed at her bonds. His meaning was clear: if she tried to escape, he would kill her. He put the knife out of reach and then untied her hands and gave her a waterskin. She drank, the water freezing all the way down. One of the others tossed him the hind leg of a rabbit they had killed, which he passed to her along with some dried corn. He observed her while she ate and then motioned toward the bushes, loosening the bonds on her ankles.

She felt numb, cold, and dirty. She stumbled a little, thankful for the use of her hands to right herself. She willed herself not to look back for her captors or the arrow that could kill her. She shuffled along, not wanting to excite her captors' suspicion. When she was about twenty yards away from them, she squatted behind a bush. Not wanting to take too long yet still hoping for an opportunity, she lingered just a moment longer than necessary. She looked ahead, off to the left, and saw the land drop away rapidly, as though it were the edge of a small cliff. She stood and stumbled back toward the warriors, observing the arrow trained on her. Her captor re-tied her hands and feet and threw a blanket over her as darkness enveloped the camp.

Will tied Dusty. He winced as he dismounted and limped over to where the mule was dying. Pulling out his knife, Will kept his revolver and the Sharps handy in case the attackers doubled back. He had to get the arrow out without falling unconscious in the process. He had no experience with such a wound but had heard stories from old soldiers involved in the Black Hawk wars. He cut a hole in the boot around where the arrow had entered, gasping from the effort. Using his cupped hands, he dumped water from the river on the wound. What if he couldn't get it out? Would he die here, alone and bleeding? He knew from the war that even minor injuries could get gangrene and, left untreated, could kill a man.

Then he thought, But I'm not alone, am I? God is with me, and also with Dove. He rested for a full minute, praying. It seemed the arrow had penetrated his ankle, between the tendon and the bone. The leather of the boots had prevented worse damage. He dug out a flask of whiskey from the saddlebag on the mule and set it handy, along with some bandages he'd brought.

Gritting his teeth, he cut around the arrowhead, gripping the shaft with both hands, pulled. The arrow came out but bleeding increased. He removed the boot and washed the wound with the freezing water and whiskey. He wrapped his ankle in bandages, applying pressure. He screamed with the pain, not caring who heard and struggled to maintain consciousness. Lightning was barking and licking his face. After perhaps ten minutes, the bleeding seemed to have stopped. Will relaxed, lying on top of the dead mule on the sandbar. It had to have been the strangest bed he'd ever had.

He wanted to get up, wanted to chase the ones that had taken Dove. But what if she was already dead? In his condition, how could he fight three warriors? What if they'd gone to a camp, a whole village? Wouldn't he just be getting himself killed? Then there was the question of whether he could even track them. Maybe Lightning could. For the millionth time, he wished for Gabe. He ate some jerky from the saddlebag and passed out.

Dawn was inching up over the horizon when he came back to himself. Cold settled into his limbs. He felt stiff, and his ankle was throbbing. He forced himself to change the blood-soaked bandage and wash the wound, then ate some more jerky, tearing off a small piece for Lightning, mindful that he needed to watch his rations. He managed to pull the damaged boot back on without breaking open the wound and hobbled over to Dusty. He untied him and let him drink. Using his knife, he cut a branch from the brush the right length to fit under his arm as a crutch. He attached hobbles to Dusty, removed his bridle, and let him move back from the stream to graze. Soon he must try mounting or give Dove up for lost.

He salvaged what he could from the dead mule's supplies. He took a swig from the whiskey to dull the pain but saved most of it to use on the wound.

The sun was still not rising high this time of year, but he judged it to be about nine in the morning when he bucked up his courage to try mounting. He had to ride—he just had to. He couldn't walk so far as back to the fort nor help Dove on foot. Dusty had wandered about thirty yards back up the trail. Will used his crutch to keep weight off the injured ankle and hefted the supplies in the other hand, his rifle slung over his shoulder.

He found a boulder about two feet tall and dropped everything beside it, then inched over to Dusty, taking his bridle from the saddlebag and putting it back on. Dusty seemed to know Will was hurt and lowered his head, whickering softly, to make the job easier. Will pulled a scarf from the bag and let Lightning smell it. It had been Dove's — he didn't know if it would help, but he figured the dog might sense something he could not.

Will sat and rested a few minutes, then removed the hobbles, grabbed the reins, and led Dusty over to the boulder. He secured everything he could to the saddle, filled the saddlebag, and put the rifle in its scabbard, praying Dusty would hold still. He clambered up on top of the boulder, holding the reins.

"Here goes." Leaning forward and grasping the pommel, he balanced on his good ankle and swung the injured one over the horse. As he found the stirrup, a shooting pain went up his leg. There would be no trotting today.

He had considered going back to the fort, asking for a cavalry troop to go out. He could get treatment and save Dove. But what were the chances that O'Brien or Carrington would send anyone for an Indian? O'Brien had let Dove have her pony, but who knew how he felt about her? After all, Dove's predicament had damaged his and his wife's reputations. He might well be happy to see her die by someone else's hand.

Dusty picked his way across the river to the other side, passing a few yards to the left of the dead mule. For some distance, the tracks were easy to follow, as the Indian ponies had galloped along, leaving plenty of sign.

Will looked up, noticing the thickening clouds. The temperature seemed to drop, and the wind was picking up. What if it snowed? How would he ever find the trail?

Will pushed Dusty into a fast walk; he had to make time while the tracks were visible. If it snowed, he'd have to make camp, build a fire, and wait it out. He had no idea where he was going, but he knew stumbling around in a whiteout made no sense. With the blinding snow, the Indians might not be moving either. At least he wouldn't be getting farther behind.

All through the morning, he followed the tracks. He was not a sufficiently experienced tracker to distinguish the tracks of Dove's pony from the others, and even if he were, they might have kept the pony and left her body in a gully. Either way, he was going on a fool's errand, but he had promised. He pushed on, cold and in pain. He didn't want to put stress on the ankle by mounting and dismounting more than necessary, so he sipped water from his canteen and munched on more jerky in the saddle.

He feared what might be happening to Dove if she was alive. He pushed her out of his head, concentrating on tracks, wondering about his family. He'd sent a letter back to his parents in Indiana, telling them where he was but had gotten no answer. He wondered if either of his sisters had had a baby yet.

The tracks were becoming fainter. Will saw that the group had stopped for a time. He rode around the muddled circle of tracks and found where they started north and east again. He looked back at the darkening sky. It began to snow.

The men had been drinking whiskey. Dove watched them, not knowing when the inevitable would come. Now that they were all awake, they talked and laughed. They removed her bonds. One of them accompanied her to gather wood for the fire. The one who'd slung her over his horse signed that she would begin the duties of his woman, his squaw. She was grateful, as long as he limited the chores to gathering wood, keeping the fire going, and cooking. She didn't want to think about after that. She knew resistance would result in death.

After the noon meal, they smoked a pipe and swapped embellished battle stories. She couldn't understand everything, just a word here and there. She listened to gauge how drunk they were and the possibility of escape. As darkness began to fall, it started to snow. Perhaps they would stay here for a time, or the snow might make the braves anxious for their winter home. It would wipe out all trace of their trail if there were any pursuit. She had scant hope of that—if Will or anyone were coming, would they not have arrived by now?

Then her captor came, binding her hands, holding a knife to her throat, and laughing. She did her best to look brave, to be ready for what must happen.

To her surprise, he bound her ankles. He moved her closer to the fire before pushing her to the ground and throwing a blanket over her.

The braves seemed very drunk. The night's ebony darkness was punctuated with snowflakes, now large ones. The moon peeked through breaks in the clouds and then hid again. Now was her best chance. After they were asleep, if she slithered away from the fire, she might get far enough to cut her bonds on a sharp rock and escape.

The fire gave enough light to see the sleeping forms around her and enough warmth to keep them from freezing. The wind had died down, and the snow swirled like feathers falling.

She began inching away from the fire. She didn't think she should try to stand yet but moved along snake-style until she was far enough away. She knew she'd leave a clear trail in the snow, but she'd worry about that later. For now, putting distance between herself and the Sioux was all that mattered.

She moved in the direction of the drop-off she'd seen, thinking to find some boulders to hide behind so she'd have time to cut her bonds. It wasn't much of a chance, but it was the only one she had.

As the light faded, the wind calmed, and in the distance, Will saw a glow—and smoke! Then the snow enveloped everything. He moved toward the smoke. The snow would be both a hindrance and a help;

they might not see him, but he wouldn't have good visibility for shooting. Maybe he should wait for dawn. He didn't know for sure yet that the fire was the people he sought. What if there were other travelers out in this storm?

The snow let up again. Will peered into the darkness at the fire, noting the rocks on three sides. There was one approach, right into the camp—they'd be watching. Unless . . . Could he climb the rocks behind them with his bad ankle? His war experience as a sniper told him that the high ground was the best and the safest. But if he did climb, could he see to make a shot? What if the wound broke open? If he waited for morning, he might freeze. He would lose the element of surprise. He knew he couldn't take even one of the warriors at close quarters. It had to be now. He stuffed his ears with cotton and put a little extra wadding in his pocket.

Will circled Dusty around to the left, coming up behind the rocks that formed the little horseshoe canyon. What to do about Lightning? What if he barked and gave him away? But he could be useful if the braves attacked. Too risky. Tying Dusty and Lightning to sagebrush, he used the rifle as a crutch, noting he would have to clean the barrel. Foot by foot, picking his way around and over rocks, Will climbed the ridge behind the camp. Scrambling for handholds, he had to crawl, slinging the rifle over his shoulder.

When he reached the top, the snow had stopped. He stayed below the line of sight and cleaned out the barrel of the Spencer. Then he moved to where he could see down into the camp. The fire illuminated three sleeping forms covered in blankets. Were they all Sioux, or was one of them Dove? At this distance, he couldn't be sure—and he had to know. What if none of them were Dove? Where was she?

There—off to the right, something was moving. The figure crawled or rolled. Not much reason for one of the braves to do that, Will thought. It must be Dove, and she must be alive. His conscience bothered him again—wasn't this just murder, sneaking up on them, shooting them in their sleep? He ignored his conscience; they'd attacked him, taken Dove. As he hesitated, one of the braves sat up, saw Dove, and ran toward her. Dove stood unsteadily and then fell down the embankment as the brave approached.

Will aimed and fired. It wasn't the most accurate shot, but the brave dropped, and the others sprang to their feet, looking both for their captive and their assailant. Will didn't hesitate long. Using the firelight and a sudden break in the clouds, he levered another round and aimed. A second brave's head exploded, blood going everywhere. The third ran behind a rock. He couldn't see Will to fire back. Just as the clouds covered the moon again, he saw the last captor making his way from rock to rock, down the slope to where Dove lay. Soon he'd be out of range, and there would be no clear shot. By the time he moved down there, it would likely be too late.

He prayed the Psalm, "Praise be to the Lord my rock, who trains my hands for war, my fingers for battle." Will waited for the warrior to pop into the open again. He had one shot, one chance. Will moderated his breathing, just like at the contest at Fort Laramie, and willed himself to be calm. There he was! Will squeezed the trigger, not jerking despite his haste. The Indian's chest opened, and he fell backward. Will waited, five seconds, ten seconds, but there was no more movement.

He stood, leaning on the rifle. He hoped the sound of the shots would not draw other hostiles. He hobbled down to Dusty, untied Lightning, and then found another rock to use as a mounting block after sheathing the rifle. Winding his way down, mindful of rocks and looking for other dangers, he rode to the bottom of the embankment beside the gully

There was Dove, bound and lying very still. There was a gash on her head and a bruise on her cheek.

Will dismounted, tied Dusty, and knelt over Dove. He touched her neck and felt a pulse. She was alive. She was breathing. He pulled out his knife and cut the thongs at her hands and ankles. What to do? He couldn't carry her. He couldn't even drag her. He had to get her to the fire and warm both of them. He breathed a prayer and then tried waving the whiskey in front of her nose, putting a drop on her lips. She responded, licking her lips, opening her eyes, and coughing.

"Dove, are you all right?"

She looked panicked, moving her head side to side, as though to see where she was. There was no recognition in her eyes, only fear.

He moved his hand toward her, and she tried to block him. She mumbled in Shoshone, but he didn't understand. It was like she didn't know who he was, didn't recognize him.

After a few minutes, she rolled over and pushed herself up to a kneeling position, facing him. She saw the horse, looked up and saw the dead Sioux that had chased her, and then back at Will. Standing, she looked puzzled, as if she were concentrating.

"Will?"

Relief flooded through him. He moved toward Dove, arms open, hopping to avoid weight on his ankle as she stood. "Dove! I thought I'd lost you."

"Head hurts bad."

She almost knocked him over as she fell into his arms.

"You came for me."

"Always."

She looked up at him, eyes searching, lips parted. He hesitated, then slowly brought his lips to hers, seeking. His heart filled with love, and then, sensing acceptance, he kissed harder, more intensely, their lips clinging together. All he could think of was how wonderful she felt, how glad he was that she was safe, how much he loved her. He felt her tremble under his touch until they parted, breathless.

Dusty made his way around and back to the campsite, where the fire still burned. Will dismounted and helped her down. She seemed unsteady, clumsy even. After he took the bridle off Dusty and tied him, he hopped over and helped Dove get blankets around her and some water to drink. For now, the snow seemed to have stopped. There were no guarantees about tomorrow, though. They'd misjudged the weather enough to come out on this trip—who knew what the next day would bring?

"Do you think you can ride?" Will asked.

"Ask me in the morning. Right now, I feel like a herd of buffalo ran over me. I was trying to escape; I remember that now."

"I'm glad you didn't get caught. But we'll need to move out at first light if you can. These warriors," he gestured to the two dead Sioux, "may have friends not far away. We can't stay here."

"I know. I wanted to go home, but we're both hurt."

"We should go back to the fort and rest. It may take a week or more to get there."

Dove agreed. They lay next to the fire. Will knew he needed to stay alert, but he also needed sleep. He trusted Lightning to stand guard. Wrapped in the same blankets, Will was lost in her hair as they nestled together. He put one arm under her head, cushioning the wound, and the other snug around her waist. She sought his hand as if for reassurance.

CHAPTER NINE

After a slow journey back to the fort with the temperature dropping, Will and Dove crossed the bridge onto the post, half-frozen. The sergeant had compassion for them and let them in. O'Brien was interested in their news of the attack and the rescue of Dove.

Will sat on a bunk while the fort surgeon looked at his ankle.

"I'd say you're mighty lucky, son. It looks like a flesh wound—a little damage to the tendons that will leave you with a limp. But you can keep the foot. I'd say you're out of danger on that score. You musta learned something about doctoring in the war."

"Yes, sir. What about Dove? She started having fever on the way back."

The doctor took off his spectacles, wiping them on his shirt, brow furrowed.

"I don't normally look at squaws. Not much point in saving them. However, I guess in this case, she did a lot of good for the women here, and the commander didn't forbid me."

He walked over to where Dove lay on the corner bunk, mumbling in Shoshone.

The doctor looked uncertain. "She . . . she won't knife me or something 'cause I'm looking her over?"

Will grabbed the crutch he'd made and hobbled over by Dove. "I can't promise anything. But I don't think she has any weapons, and from the look of her, not much strength either. I'll stay by her side while you look."

The doctor muttered something and put his hand on her forehead. He brought a candle closer to look at her head wound. Her eyes opened, flashing at him, and then she seemed to relax at seeing Will.

"This is the doctor, the medicine man. He's going to see where you're hurt. Let him look."

105

Dove looked from one to the other and gave a barely perceptible nod.

The doctor lifted her arms one at a time, then asked her to move her eyes, following his finger.

"I'm going to touch your body—I'm just trying to see if you have broken bones. If it hurts, tell me or yell. I mean you no harm. I'm not trying to hurt you. Understand?"

Dove nodded.

The doctor applied light pressure, running his hands along her head, neck, and shoulders. He skipped over her breasts, instead feeling the sides and the ribs just below them.

"Aiee!" Dove exclaimed.

The doctor stopped. "I'm going to do that again. If it hurts, yell out."

She yelped in pain.

The doctor continued, examining the outer bones of the pelvis, upper leg, lower leg, ankles, and feet.

He turned to Will. "Well, your friend here has a low fever. Pretty common in cases like hers. Not much I can do for her. If you get one of the women over here, she's got a broken seventh rib, right side; they could have her take a deep breath to expand the rib cage, then tape it to hold it and help it heal. She's had a nasty knock to the head. Keep the wound clean, bathe it with alcohol—whiskey I can prescribe!" He laughed. "She may have trouble remembering things for a while. Keep her still and quiet. Within a couple of weeks, she ought to feel better."

They were back to waiting again.

Both Will and Dove improved as May wound down. There was great excitement in the fort—the government and the Sioux were holding a council. A treaty proposed to Red Cloud, Man Afraid of His Horses, and other influential Sioux would offer a chance of peace.

Will woke and stretched. Pulling on his shirt, he stood and got coffee going on the stove. He pushed aside the hanging blanket and walked over to wake Dove on her side of the room.

"There's a lot of horses and men out there. Why don't we take a slow walk around the fort and see what's going on? The fresh air might do you good."

She stretched and rolled over, ignoring him. He let her rest awhile and then tried again, tempting her with coffee and breakfast.

Dove smiled and said, "Why do we care about who comes? It's cold. I still don't feel strong." She sighed. "But I can see you are stubborn and curious. All right, I'll walk with you. But you owe me extra sleep tomorrow."

After they ate, Will helped her outside. They met Clarissa, who was coming to their cabin and began a slow circuit of the fort. Will saw Dove tense; there was a new reason to be afraid. There were hundreds if not thousands of Sioux camped around the fort. She would not dare go outside its protection.

"Will, I'm afraid. There are so many Sioux around, so many enemies. If they attack, the soldiers cannot stop them, I think. How will I ever get home?"

He sat next to her, putting his arm around her shoulders.

"I wish I had answers, but we must be patient. I am praying, and God will show us the right time."

"How do you know your God even cares about me? I've seen white men before that called on their God, but it did not keep them from lying to my people or trying to kill them. Washakie says the whites do not tell the truth because most don't know-how. You seem different."

"Thanks."

Dove looked serious. "You have a lot to learn about my people."

"I guess I'd better start, then," Will replied, pulling her into a kiss. She allowed him but then pulled away and whacked him playfully.

"See? Even squaws can be dangerous."

The next two days passed with tension thick around the fort. Will saw the US Second Cavalry, and portions of the Eighteenth Infantry marched in as June began, acting as reinforcements.

For days, gossip whirled through the fort as the Indians and the army officers bargained, the Sioux stubbornly resisting opening the Bozeman Trail, the army giving concessions but insistent on creating new forts farther into the Bighorn country.

Dove and Will were sitting down to a simple lunch of rabbit and buffalo tongue when the door to their little room swung open.

"Got enough for an old man? I'm tuckered out listening to the soldiers."

"Gabe! When did you get here?"

"Just about an hour ago. I was about to go back to St. Louis when I got word of these new forts. They persuaded me to come along, scout for them. Not sure it was a good idea—they had already cut my pay in half! Still, I druther be in the mountains than just about anywhere. And I remembered my promise to see Washakie again."

He sobered. "There's gonna be trouble for sure. Them army types, they don't understand anything. Carrington came in with orders to build new forts in the Bighorn, Indians, or no Indians. Red Cloud and Man Afraid of His Horses already left. They say that the white man parleys, but he lies—asking permission to build the forts but then saying he will steal the land regardless of what the Sioux say."

"Can they do that?"

"Looks like they aim to try. Red Cloud, he's not one the army should get riled. But Carrington is going west in just a few days. Taking women and children too. This whole country, from here to the Yellowstone, gonna be crawling with cussed Sioux, mad as grizzlies and ready to lift your hair. Carrington's better than most—he listens, at least sometimes. If'n you want to go west, get to Washakie, might as well go along. No road's going to be safe for a good while. Might as well let the soldiers shoot for you."

Will filled him in on their attempt to go west and their encounter with the Sioux.

"Sounds like you're lucky to have kept your hair! Well, the Sioux have no love for me. More'n a few would like to have my scalp outside their lodges."

Will and Dove talked for a few minutes, then turned back to Gabe, who was busy devouring the buffalo tongue.

"We'll go if Colonel Carrington will have us. As long as you'll see us to Washakie when you can."

"That I'll do," said Gabe.

The following morning, Will and Dove accompanied Gabe to see Colonel Henry Carrington. They decided to let Gabe do the talking.

"Colonel Carrington, sir? A minute of your time, please? These two young'uns would like to accompany your expedition west. The feller here, Will Crump, was a Confederate lieutenant in the war, and I ain't never seen a better shot. The gal here is a niece to old Washakie, and she's just trying to get back home to her people. She might come in handy if we run into any Shoshone. Washakie's band is friendly, but if we hit Bannock's or Pocatello's band, it won't be as purty. I'd vouch for both of them."

Carrington's intelligent black eyes probed Will and Dove. He stroked his full beard in thought.

"How do we know that this young woman won't betray us?"

Gabe looked as a father might, explaining the world to his naive son. "Sir, Dove here is Eastern Shoshone. I've known her uncle for twenty years. The Sioux, the Cheyenne, and the Arapaho all hate

Shoshone. She ain't about to help 'em. The fact is she's afeared of 'em—that's why she wants to tag along with us."

Carrington considered, turning to Will. "You the one I hear about? The one who outshot one of Berdan's sharpshooters?"

Will was a little embarrassed but spoke up. "Yes, sir. Though he was a fine shot, sir."

"What unit were you with in the war?"

"Second Kentucky, sir. General Morgan's cavalry."

"Crump, did you say? Did you have a sister—a Miss Albinia Crump in the Underground Railroad?"

Will raised his eyebrows in surprise. "Yes, sir. Begging your pardon, but how would you know Albinia?"

"I headed up a group for the army working against the Knights of the Golden Circle in Indiana. Her name came up a few times. Brave girl."

He turned back to Gabe. "All right. They can come, but you're responsible for them. Maybe the squaw—Dove, did you say? Maybe she can help with the children and some of the work about camp. Better than starving here in the squaw village yonder with the other abandoned Indian women. Be ready at first light."

The next morning, the procession started. Gabe and a couple of Pawnee scouts went first, followed by the supply wagons hauling tools, food, and other necessities for building the forts. There were several hundred in the group, including a few women and children. Carrington sent a company of cavalry off ahead to Fort Reno. Dove brought up the rear, riding next to Will. She thought she'd be able to stand the trip—these soft whites would never travel at the speed of Shoshone warriors. Everyone except Gabe and Dove seemed to expect smooth travel; the treaty was in force with Spotted Tail and a few other Sioux chiefs. The telegraph said that the newspapers back east were trumpeting peace and an end to the Indian troubles.

Dove grew tired on the journey. Her head still ached at times, and her breathing rasped due to her still-healing rib. She saw occasional indications of watchers—mirrors flashing on the heights, wildlife scuttering as though avoiding other intruders—and while it frightened her, she rested in the knowledge that Wolf would protect her, along with Will and Gabe. Some of the soldiers were brave men. Still, she knew if Red Cloud and his Bad Faces decided to attack in force, their train would be no match for them. The idea of her carrying a pistol made the other whites nervous, so she carried a two-shot derringer that Will had gotten for her at the sutler. If Sioux attacked, one shot could always be for herself.

She looked over at Will and smiled. He smiled back and resumed scanning the forest and ridges, always on the lookout for trouble, hands alert and his seat on the buckskin secure, like a warrior used to surprises.

They were still shy when alone together, not sharing the same tent or a bed, though everyone thought they did. She wondered how long it would take him to come around to it. Maybe she should suggest it? White men were odd. If they ever made it home, would her father let her marry a white man? What if Will never asked her? What if her father wouldn't consider a courtship? Would the tribal council even allow that? So many questions without answers. She would not think of it now. She would enjoy the blue sky, the wind on her face, and the memory of his kiss, his embrace, holding her by the fire. The other white men did not seem to touch their women, not where anyone could see.

Noon was approaching, and they paused in the shade of some trees near the Platte River. She was tired of the white man's food. She slid down from her pony, wincing a little as she hit the ground but not willing to wait for Will's assistance. He'd ask what she was doing, and she wanted to surprise him.

Dove checked her surroundings. Finding herself alone, she looked among the trees. She spied the roots she wanted: wild potatoes.

Along with a few other herbs growing nearby and some dried rabbit from their saddlebags, she soon had a stew boiling that tempted some other women.

Soon they arrived at the old Fort Conner, renamed Fort Reno, where Will had been the previous fall. Carrington relieved the volunteer garrison, sending the men south to muster out and replacing them with regulars of the Eighteenth Infantry. Will and Dove camped in their tents for the next week while the soldiers cut timber and built walls and towers at the four corners of the stockade, providing a welcome respite from worries about an attack.

Will began to keep a journal, as much for something to do as anything else. It had been over a year since he'd set out from Indiana traveling west. He wondered again about his family. He sighed. He supposed that was the price he paid, coming west away from everyone he knew. Recently, since his time with Dove and growing closer to her, the dreams that haunted his sleep had become less frequent and not as fearful. Some nights he dreamed of boyhood on the farm before the war when his worst problem was getting the day's chores done.

Dove's health seemed to improve, and other than being fatigued and irritable, her overall condition seemed to be better. He wondered what would happen if she got home—when she got home, he corrected himself. What did the future hold for them? He grew to love her more each day, but he did not want it to be a cheap white man-squaw relationship such as he had seen at the fort. He gathered she did not have the same scruples about sharing a bed that he did, yet he did not want to take advantage of her, to treat her with any less respect and dignity than he would want another man to do with one of his sisters.

June gave way to July. One morning, Gabe came over to talk to Will and Dove.

"Seems the colonel thinks he's done all the damage he can here. A couple of Cheyenne came near the post yesterday with the message that they's willing for the soldiers to be here, providing they don't go any farther up the trail and don't build no more forts. They say the Sioux mean business: build those forts, and it will be all-out war. Says they're off doing Sun Dances now, getting organized. Carrington says he has his orders and sent 'em packing. Guess the next legs may not be as peaceful. Colonel says we're heading out today, leaving two companies here to defend this fort."

"I guess that gets us farther west, but where would Washakie's band be from here?"

"Hard to say exactly, 'cept most likely south. It'll be a couple of months yet before they move to the winter range. Prob'ly hunting buffalo, storing up for the winter."

"We're getting closer but farther away?"

Gabe shifted a little. "Yep. But we're getting farther west, with pretty good protection. Even Red Cloud ain't likely to take on this big of a train, I reckon. He'll bide his time or take little bits here and there. Anyhow, I must see this train through—you oughta understand about that. Once he builds his forts, we can find our way to Washakie."

Will looked at Dove. "If we make it that far . . ."

It took a while to get the command moving, though there were fewer of them than on the previous march. It was almost midday before they set out.

They made camp near the North Platte, ready to cross the next day. With the sun peeking above the ridge, Will was considering making a fire when he heard gunshots.

Grabbing his rifle and coming out of the tent, he saw Major Heymond running about, shouting orders.

"After them! At this rate, we'll have no horses left!"

Gabe spoke up, "Hold it! You ain't gonna catch them cussed Sioux, and you'll lose men. They want you to follow 'em."

The major glared at Gabe. "You forget yourself. I give the orders here."

The major mounted with his squad and chased the retreating Sioux, who were driving horses and mules before them, having overcome the picket guard set to watch them. The guard still had his hair, and although stunned from the war club that had hit his head, he appeared otherwise unhurt as he wobbled toward the makeshift hospital.

Carrington delayed their departure, waiting for the major's return. An hour or so later, a lone rider galloped into camp, his horse lathered and wheezing.

"Colonel! Colonel! They're trapped and surrounded. Two hundred Injuns. You gotta send help!"

Carrington looked alarmed. "Captain, take two companies of infantry and fifty cavalry and go to Major Heymond's relief. Double time!"

Gabe threw up his hands, frustrated.

"Colonel, if you let 'em, the Sioux gonna draw you into a fight you can't win. They're just testing you now, seeing what you'll risk for a few missing horses. If you wanna make it to the Bighorn country, you got to set more guards, not chase off on fool's errands, as the major done. You hired me to guide and advise—I can't help you if you don't listen."

Carrington considered. "All right, my friend. Your advice has been accurate, and you are too valuable to this mission to lose. We'll play it your way. I'll order everyone to stay close to camp, put out double or triple pickets at night."

In the early afternoon, the soldiers sent out returned.

"Sir, we were surrounded, backed up to a creek. We retreated and found the remains of an emigrant train, all dead. Sir, it was some of the emigrants we saw at Fort Reno. We found these," he gestured at an Indian woman and five children, "in the brush, hiding. She says her husband was white, one of the ones killed," Heymond reported.

"What shall we do with them?"

"Sir, they beg to return to Fort Reno. As it is half a day's ride, I suggest sending them back with one or two men for an escort. If attacked, the men can do their best but abandon them if it's necessary to save themselves."

Will fumed but said nothing. Hadn't Carrington heard anything Gabe said about fool's errands?

"All right, Major. Pick two men, but have them rejoin us as soon as possible. Send one of the Pawnee with them if they don't object to helping her."

Will looked over at Dove, eyebrows raised. When they'd retreated a short distance, he asked her, "Why would anyone not help the poor woman? She's terrified and has those children."

"She's Sioux," Dove said.

Will rode next to Gabe for the remainder of the trip and encouraged Dove to make friends with the other women—it might be a long winter if they did not get along. Sometimes he and Gabe were gone all day. They made camp on Lake De Smet while Carrington considered where to build the fort to be known as Fort Carrington.

"Colonel, I'm telling you, you need to put the fort more in the open, away from these hills. There's nice valley yonder, where you can see riders approach from all sides for some distance."

"Gabe, I appreciate what you're saying, but I must insist that we be closer to water and to the forest, else we must haul the timber too far. I'm thinking just near the Piney there. Yes, I think that will do very well. I'll send a company north to scout another fort location on the Bighorn. We'll start construction at once."

Gabe walked away, muttering about "dern fool tenderfeet."

The construction did begin in earnest the next day, with axes ringing through the forested area. Like needles on a porcupine, the eight-foot stockade wall began to rise around an area of about seventeen acres. Barracks, mess hall, flagpole, and powder magazine took shape with all the speed the few hundred men could manage.

Will couldn't figure why the Sioux didn't strike before they finished the fort, but aside from pretending to be wolves, sneaking into the corral, and making off with horses, they did not attack the main body. The wood train almost always had a skirmish before arriving back at the fort. Even Will could see the mirrors flashing on the hills, the signal fires, and other evidence of Sioux presence.

He decided to ask Gabe about it.

"Why don't they get a large group and attack? Before the soldiers finish the fort?"

"A head-on battle ain't their style. Besides, Red Cloud, cuss his hide, is a whole lot smarter than these paper-collar soldiers think. He wants to lure out smaller parties of soldiers where he has the advantage of surprise, knowing the country, and away from those," he said, pointing at the mountain howitzers already mounted on platforms. "You fought in the war; you know what a load of canister shot from those can do. Most of the Sioux don't have rifles—just arrows, knives, tomahawks, and clubs. And they sure don't have cannons. They call 'em the guns that shoot twice because they boom, and then the canisters explode grapeshot in all directions. Besides, they count it an honor to get up close to their enemy, expose themselves to real danger, even touch an enemy before they kill him. Long-distance doesn't carry the same idea of bravery. They call it counting coup."

Will nodded. "I heard about some battles in the war at the end, where men couldn't fight back. No ammunition and up against Yankee cannon. It sounds somewhat similar. Except no charging and frontal assaults."

Dove found the white women unreceptive to her presence. They weren't mean; they just didn't notice she existed—she might as well have been a tree. She'd expected nothing more but tried for Will's sake. The one redeeming grace was Clarissa, whom she had discovered was in the group. Clarissa had ridden in her father's supply wagon with her mother and so was separated from the other women and children traveling in the ambulance. Clarissa's father seemed to melt into a grudging acceptance of Dove after the trial.

Dove knew that as out of place as she felt with the whites, Will would feel equally out of place with her people.

She watched him with Old Gabe; they seemed to have forged a friendship. Gabe was so unusual—a white man who respected the traditions and beliefs of her people yet was comfortable in the white world. Some would not think him good because of his association with the soldiers. Yet he bridged the two worlds, something Washakie found valuable. The whites never saw any difference between tribes. To most whites, all were just savages, "dirty Injuns." Even among Shoshone, there were differences—the sheep eaters, the seed eaters, the groundhog eaters, united by language and culture but with local variations.

She saw Will laughing with Gabe. Dove cared for Will, but with the tensions on the trail, they didn't seem to laugh together as much anymore. At first, she just smiled and was grateful for his protectiveness, his concern for her safety. She had lived in these mountains and plains all her life. As she healed, she grew more restless. He was like a young boy, struck by wonder and caution at things that were new to him. She was used to roaming with her band, having a home that moved with the familiar rhythm of the seasons. He seemed to want to find one spot and stay there.

Dove went back to lining the moccasins she was making with

rabbit fur for the coming winter. She'd deal with the future a day at a time.

Will grew bored just sitting around, riding with Gabe on scout expeditions that always yielded sign of Sioux but no actual conflict, and just waiting. It reminded him far too much of the winter camps during the war. He asked to join one of the work crews, chopping lumber and building the fort, to have something to do. Dove always seemed busy and, lately, more distant. Women! One minute wanting your attention and love, the next some undiscoverable thing made them push you away. He began to wonder how he'd let his guard down. Hadn't he learned anything from his experience with Jenny?

Will looked over plans for the fort. The stables and hay yard were near the Piney Creek, along with the teamsters' quarters, mess, and wood yard. A gate led to the creek for water collection, and a set of interior gates linked this annex to the main fort. The main area had as its center the round magazine with a large flagpole on top. There was a cavalry yard for practice, adjoined by the cavalry horses' stables. The officers' quarters were on the south side, and the hospital and chapel were next to those buildings. At the north side of the parade ground were the band quarters, the sutler, Carrington's office, and the guardhouse. In the northwest corner were the bakery and the regular soldiers' barracks, north to south on the west end. The main gates were on the north wall. The sawmill brought from Nebraska was outside the fort. Blockhouses sat at diagonal corners and had mountain howitzers placed in them for elevation and range. Other guns and more massive cannons were on the southwest corner of the parade ground.

Day by day, the buildings and walls rose despite constant threats to the wood train that brought logs for the construction.

Carrington approached Will. "Crump, I've got a problem. One

of the men is sick, normally rides guard for the wood train. Would you be willing to fill in?"

"Don't see why not."

"Good, good. They'll be moving out in five minutes."

Will grabbed his two rifles and checked the load on his pistol. He approached the wagons, finding the other guard was Bill Hurst, his opponent in the shooting match.

Hurst looked at him in disgust. "Got us a Johnny Reb to nursemaid."

Will's lips thinned. He replied, "General Carrington thought you might need some help."

Hurst said, "We might at that—but I don't see any."

Will mounted the wagon box, stowing the Sharps and keeping the Spencer at the ready. Hurst rode in the second wagon. Five mounted soldiers accompanied them. They drove northeast from the fort toward the wooded foothills. Will scanned everywhere, looking for trouble. After about two miles, they came upon stumps of trees created by the previous logging. Will got down and took up a position behind some rocks. Hurst glanced at him and then moved to the trees. The soldiers unloaded axes and saws and got to work.

Will saw a mirror flash on the opposite ridge, and then, ahead on the road, three ponies appeared with mounted warriors. They were just out of range for the Spencer. The warriors waved lances in the air, riding back and forth, but they were careful to stay out of range. They kept this up for an hour. Will thought they must be trying to trick the soldiers into going after them.

The soldiers finished loading the wagons with new cut wood. Will and Hurst mounted, and the wagons turned back for the fort. Each had a team of two horses. They had gone about a hundred yards when Will saw a flash from the forest on the left. Arrows whizzed and landed in the wood and the wagons. The teamsters urged the horses forward, and the wagon bounced crazily, making aim difficult. He crouched behind one of the logs, looking backward, trying to see where assailants were hiding. He saw a brave up in a tree and fired.

The wagon jostled just as his finger squeezed the trigger—he'd missed! Another arrow whined in front of him. What if they got the horses? He aimed the Spencer again—this time the Sioux fell from the tree. He heard cracks from Hurst's rifle as well. He levered another cartridge, sought another target, but none presented itself. The fort gates opened, and they were inside, safe.

Dove was growing restless. She collected roots and berries daily, and taught Will their names when he returned to their tents, worn out from the day's work.

They seemed to have fallen into a routine, like an older married couple.

The next day, she saw Gabe mounting up. She ran over to him.

"Please, Gabe. I'm about to go crazy in this fort. Can I not come with you today? I'm only a woman, but I do know some about tracking and the Sioux. Just don't tell Will—he'd think it too dangerous."

The old man raised his eyebrows and one corner of his mouth. Then he looked at her pleading face and said, "Why not? Get your pony and come along. I'm just going to the top of Pilot Hill to have a look-see." His blue eyes twinkled.

Dove got her pony and was ready in less than five minutes. She still had her derringer tucked in her clothes, and she also had a bow with a quiver of arrows and her knife.

Gabe chuckled at her armament. He spoke to her in Shoshone. "You got twice the sense of some of them settler folk. I don't need to tell you to go quiet. They're out there, sure enough. We want to get an idea of how many lodges and whether it's just Sioux or maybe some Cheyenne and Arapahoe too."

Dove nodded and followed him, riding out the side gate by the chapel. Gabe signaled her in that direction.

"I figger they're watching the main gate. They might be watching the side too. If you see mirror flashes that I don't, make a sound like a baby red-tailed hawk."

She nodded. Gabe rode in front. The wind was dry and whipped her black hair around. They did not talk anymore, each concentrating, listening, and watching for any sign of an ambush. They moved northwest from the fort, crossing Piney Creek. The water came up to the horses' knees and had a sound footing on the bottom.

Less than an hour later, they approached the top of Pilot Hill and dismounted. They stayed off the skyline, out of sight. The sun was about a quarter of the way up in the sky, and it wasn't hot yet.

Dove saw the tracks first and motioned to Gabe.

Gabe whispered, "Looks like about twenty. Some Sioux, some Cheyenne, by the moccasin prints and the arrow fletch over there. Maybe two days ago?"

"Yes. They are not far away."

Gabe crawled to where he could see over the edge down into the valley. Dove followed. She saw a slight hint of smoke on another hill, maybe two hundred yards away, and pointed to it. Gabe acknowledged and looked at the sun. He signed it was time to get back to the fort.

They had barely ridden through the gate by the chapel when they heard the bugler blow "to horse," and the cavalry troops scrambled, mounted, and moved out the front entrance. Dove wondered at the commotion and whether it had anything to do with the tracks they'd seen.

She didn't have long to wait. The soldiers returned, yelling, "Open the gates!" They escorted five wagons moving at a gallop. The teams came to a halt, safe inside the fort. The mountain howitzers boomed twice, causing the pursuing Sioux to retreat.

Dove noticed the horses on the wagon teams lathered and heaving. "What are the crazy white people doing? Don't they know the Sioux will attack them?"

Gabe shook his head. "Heading for the goldfields and free

land. My guess is most of 'em never saw Sioux or any other Injun before and think they're all tame. Guess they learned different." He pointed at two arrows stuck in the wooden sides of the wagons.

Will came running out of their quarters to see what the problem was. The wagon train inhabitants were beginning to emerge, stepping down from their wagons. Everyone was talking at once. Children wailed, and dogs barked, running in circles.

"I thought they'd catch us and scalp us right there! This was supposed to be safe!"

Will walked over to help just as a blond woman, alone in the party, was looking for a way to get down without ripping her dress. Will offered his hand and helped her down.

"Thank you, kind sir. I thought we'd never make it."

"Have you anyone to help you with your things?"

"No, no, it's just me. I've come west to start over—headed for San Francisco or Oregon." She dabbed at her eyes with a handkerchief. "But now I don't know what I'll do . . . Those awful Indians! I was terrified."

Will dropped her hand. "You may not be aware, ma'am, but this is their home, their country—you're the foreigner. I understand that you're terrified, but you must have known there would be dangers on the trail."

She laughed. "Oh, yes. Dangers from men. Maybe from the weather. But I wasn't expecting to be chased and threatened with murder. The newspapers in the East all say the Indian troubles are over. I think they need to visit here . . ."

"Perhaps. Fortunately, you weren't hurt. Why did you come west?"

"To start over, as I said. I was . . . in business, and the business failed. I'm hoping to try again. I'm an entertainer." She startled when she caught sight of Dove watch her. "What is that . . . that savage doing in the fort? Didn't we escape them?"

"That is my friend, Dove. An Eastern Shoshone. Enemy of the Sioux that chased you."

"Well, I suppose with men like yourself about, I have nothing to fear. Mister . . . ?"

"Crump. Will Crump."

"Pleased to meet you. I'm Miss Delilah Simmons, lately of St. Louis."

When Will returned to the cabin, it was after dark. Dove was on her bunk on the wall opposite his, apparently asleep. She hadn't left a lamp or candle for him, as she usually did if he was out late, which was odd. He went to bed quietly and soon was dreaming.

He thrashed about, hearing cannon, shouted orders, seeing a young Yankee in the sights of his Whitworth. The Yankee turned toward him, and the face became his father's. Something came toward him, and he lashed out, thinking it was a bayonet. Dove's startled cry of pain brought him awake. The room was dark, with only dim moonlight.

He'd hit her as she leaned over him.

"Were you dreaming again? The war?"

"Yes . . . yes, dreaming. But what are you doing?"

"I was coming to your bed. Let me comfort you. I love you, no matter what."

She bent and covered his attempted protest in a kiss, her softness brushing against him. When she released his lips, he protested.

"No! Not like this."

She kissed him again, desperately this time.

Will grabbed both her arms and pushed her back, gently but firmly.

"No, I said."

Dove had tears in her eyes. "You don't want me?"

"I want you. Just . . . just not like this. I want you to be happy, to be with me always. Just not this way, not now. I can't—my faith won't let me. I'll talk to your father when we get you home."

Dove stamped over to the hook where her dress hung. She slipped it over her head and put on her moccasins. Instead of returning to Will, she lifted the latch, threw the door open, and ran out into the night.

CHAPTER TEN

Will searched everywhere in the fort for Dove, but there was no sign. He went to Gabe.

"Dove is missing. We had a little misunderstanding." He related the incident of the previous night.

"Lovers' quarrel, eh? I've had a few. Shoshone don't see the whole marriage thing the way white people do. Joining together doesn't necessarily mean marriage, though often the gal's papa sees it that way. And marriage is as simple as the father's consent and the exchange of some gifts. No white dress and church wedding—no ceremony at all. Just papa's consent and moving to the same lodge. Some Shoshone have more than one wife, like the Mormons or the Crow."

"The culture lesson is nice, Gabe, but what do I do? Don't you understand? She's gone! She could be dead out there."

"Son, you're getting better at seeing, and I'm getting worse. My eyes ain't what they used to be a year ago. Ain't no use looking for her. Either she's dead, or she's alive and hiding better'n you'll ever find her. No sense in us both losing our hair over it. Won't help."

"But I have to do something!"

"Well, for starters, I don't put a lotta stock in it, but you're big on God . . . You could pray. Beyond that, the next time a company goes out, volunteer to be an extra gun. Lord knows they could use you. But you know where the big hill is, the one called Lodge Trail Ridge? Don't go beyond there, no matter what the soldiers do. You could go out with them, keep your eyes peeled. She'll come back on her own after she cools down, or she won't. Is her pony still in the corral? If not, she could be twenty miles from here."

Will checked the corral and saw Dove's pony munching oats. Relieved, he knew she must not be far away. Will strode off toward Carrington's office. Delilah was coming out of the sutler's.

"Good day, Mr. Crump! You seem in a hurry today."

Will stopped, not wanting to be rude. "Yes, ma'am. I have to find my friend. I must speak to the colonel."

"That squaw girl? Surely you can't be serious. Why would the colonel bother about her? For that matter, why do you?"

"She saved my life, more than once, if it's any of your business."

"My, my. Testy today, are we? Well, if it means that much to you, by all means. But you could take the time to get to know me."

Will almost dropped his jaw, then squared it. "My apologies, Miss Simmons. Another time, perhaps? I have pressing business at the moment."

Will knocked at Carrington's door.

"Enter."

"Sir. I want to report Dove missing."

"Who?"

"Dove, my Shoshone friend. She disappeared last night. I'm worried about her."

Carrington snorted. "Gone over to the other side, I shouldn't wonder. I never thought it was a good idea to bring her along. Good riddance, I say. I have neither men, time, nor horses to waste on looking for some Indian who looks just like a hundred others trying to kill us. Now, if that is all, I have more important matters to attend to."

Will held his anger in check. "All right, then. When is there an expedition going out?"

"Expedition? None that I—"

Just then, an aide burst into the office.

"Sir! It's the wood train, sir. Pilot Hill signals an Indian attack."

"Blast it all to creation! If only we didn't need more wood . . ."

Will remembered Gabe telling the colonel about the problems with the location of the fort and Carrington not listening. He thought it best to be silent on that score under the circumstances.

"All right. Get Fetterman and Grummond. They've been bothering me to death about fighting Indians—let them get their chance. Sound Boots and Saddles! Saddle my horse; I'll personally command a company. Fly, man! No time to lose."

The aide ran out to obey.

"Sir . . ."

"You still here? I've no time to worry about your Indian. For all I know, she led the hostiles to the wood party."

"Permission to accompany the troops, sir. To rescue the wood wagon."

"Thought you didn't want to fight anymore, boy? Well, I know you can shoot, or at least Gabe says you can. We'll likely need all the guns we can get. But I take no responsibility for you, understand? Now go, if you're coming. We leave in five minutes."

"Yes, sir!" Will snapped a salute.

Will saddled Dusty. As he came out onto the parade ground, he saw Clarissa. On impulse, he stopped to talk to her.

"Where are you going?" she asked.

"I'm going to find Dove and help out this troop, add a little protection."

Clarissa shook her head. "I don't know whether I should tell you, but last night I saw her go out the side gate by the chapel. I didn't want to say anything because some people here would think she was meeting with the Sioux, even though that's crazy."

Will was even more determined. "Then she's out there somewhere, and I'm going to find her."

"I'll pray for you."

"Will you watch Lightning for me? I don't think it's a good idea for him to come along. Too much potential for shooting."

"I'll make sure he doesn't follow you."

Will saw the others mounting and waved as he swung up into the saddle. He fully intended to look as best he could for Dove while guarding the soldiers. His object was not to do battle, but he would defend himself or any soldiers he saw under attack.

He watched Captain Fetterman trot through the gate with two companies of infantry and part of Lieutenant Bingham's cavalry.

Once ready, Will joined Carrington and Lieutenant Grummond, along with about thirty cavalry troops.

He rode up to Grummond. "Sir, if acceptable to you, I will take the rear guard. I often protected my troop that way in the war."

"I'll bet you did, Reb. And probably the first to run too," returned Grummond. "Well, I intend to be upfront in case the fighting starts. Suit yourself, Reb."

Will stared after him and shook his head. Some folks just couldn't let it go.

The column moved out, Will trailing at the rear. He looked for any sign that might offer itself, a piece of clothing, something that belonged to Dove. His heart pounded with love and worry—he had to find her. It was freezing, and the ground was hard. If Dove was out here, he figured she stood little chance of survival unless someone rescued her and got her back to safety.

He wished Gabe were well and going with him. He followed the column until they crested the summit between the fort and Lodge Trail Ridge. Will decided there wasn't a better place short of the ridge itself and dismounted, tying Dusty to a tree and moving behind a stand of rocks. From here, he could cover the soldiers and have a broad view of the valley below, all the way to Lodge Trail Ridge.

He pulled out his rifle, checked his pistol one more time, and settled down to wait. The soldiers moved ahead down the trail.

Rifle shots rang out through the winter air. Will looked toward the sound and made out soldiers, probably Fetterman's group, ahead and to the east, almost at the top of the ridge. A large number of Indians on horseback circled the soldiers. He could faintly hear the war cries, being about half a mile distant—too far for him to shoot, even with his scope. Carrington's column was moving up from the south to assist them. Will saw no current danger to Carrington. He concentrated on the scene in front of him. Creeping forward and staying low, Will reached an outcropping where his rifle could reach the fight. Just as he settled the gun on a rock, he looked left, seeing an arrow peeking out of the dark trees, pointed at him.

Will whirled, rolling to a prone position while drawing his revolver. He aimed, cocked, saw the arrow leave the string. The arrow sang through the air over his head. The arrow pierced the heart of an Indian, who fell on top of him from behind, spoiling his aim. He nearly dropped the revolver. The shaft in the Indian snapped as its butt hit his back, and a war club clattered uselessly to the ground. Will pushed off the fallen warrior, firing once when he was clear, then rolled right to aim and fire again at the one with the bow. Finger on the trigger, he saw Dove step forward from behind the tree, holding the bow loose in her hands. He uncocked the revolver.

He lay breathing hard, not sure what was next, but realizing she had saved him.

Dove dropped the bow and ran toward him, arms open wide. Will stood, holstered his gun, and just held her, willing time to stand still. He wanted to stand forever, just feeling her softness, smelling her hair. No complications, no decisions, only the two of them.

Renewed sounds of battle interrupted his reverie.

"Dove, I'm so sorry. I love you. I never meant to hurt you or put you in danger. When you left, I realized all I cared about is you. If you'd been killed . . ."

"It's all right now. I should never have run. I'm just glad I was here when you needed me. But we should go. We'll have time for more talk later. There could be more Sioux about, and I hear the soldiers fighting."

"Should we go and help them?"

"Not me. I owe the blue coats nothing. Soldiers have been only misery for my people and me. You go if you must, but I hope you will go with me . . . back to the fort, then when the weather is good, to my people."

Will felt torn, but he'd come to search for Dove, only promising to help the soldiers to look for her safely. Now that he'd found her, was he willing to risk them both?

"Give me five minutes. Do you have more arrows? Guard my back. I'll do what I can from here."

Returning to his rock and picking up the Sharps, he saw the cavalry had retreated much closer, with many mounted Indians in pursuit. He saw a man fall sideways out of his saddle. An arrow hit his horse in the neck, and the horse landed on top of him. The lead Sioux stopped, dismounted, and made ready to scalp the trooper.

Making range and wind calculations from habit, Will judged it to be about six hundred yards. He took careful aim and fired—once, twice. The Indian dropped his scalping knife and fell. A trooper circled back, dismounted, and pulled his companion free, putting him on the horse and jumping on ahead of him.

Dove tugged on Will just as he was readying another shot on the first Sioux pursuers. He fired anyway as the Indians released a volley of arrows and musket balls at the retreating troops. Will missed. A trooper at the rear fell backward out of the saddle, a lance in his back.

Quickly he mounted and pulled Dove up behind him on Dusty. They rode back to the safety of the fort.

Shortly after they returned, the wood train and the soldiers came in, bearing the bodies of Lieutenant Bingham and Sergeant Bowers. Grummond appeared shaken—though he did shoot a venomous look at Will and Dove, as though thinking Will a coward. They later learned seven Sioux had confronted him after going with Bingham farther than Carrington had ordered.

Will joined Dove in their cabin.

"We need to talk about what happened." He put a hand on each shoulder, turning her toward him.

She stopped scraping the hide in her hands. She looked up at Will and shook her head.

"No, nothing needs to be said. That is the problem with white people. You talk too much about things that should not be said and get into trouble with your many words."

"But you ran away . . . and you saved my life again."

"Would you not have done the same for me?"

"Of course, but—"

"Then, nothing more is needed." She dropped the hide and came to him. He took her in his arms, and she snuggled closer. "You said you love me. If you do, you will come with me to my father. When spring comes, we will see if you still feel the same."

"I do not change easily. I look forward to it."

He reached up to cup her face with both hands and brushed her lips with his. He looked into her eyes and then kissed her harder. Her arms encircled him, and they fell back together, just holding each other.

Will noticed that Dove was not eating much. He wondered what was troubling her. Since the rescue and their time afterward, she seemed withdrawn. What could he have done to offend her?

Gabe knocked on the door and came in complaining of the cold, which Will thought unlike him.

"What's the matter with you two young'uns? Are your tongues frozen? I can't seem to get the cold out of these bones."

"The Sioux attacked the wood party again. Do you think it's safe to go out and look for a deer?"

"Sioux out there are thicker than the snow. Don't know why

they haven't gone to winter camp. Not like 'em. It makes me nervous. It's like they quit scrapping with each other and all united against the soldiers. No, I wouldn't set foot outside the fort less'n you have to. Sutler's still got beans and cornmeal. Wouldn't find much deer anyway, this cold. Deer don't move around much, find a food source, and stay by it. Soldiers, they got to go, but it ain't worth your hair to go out."

Will went to get wood for the fire and saw today's wood train getting ready to go out of the fort. He wondered at the size of the escort—did Carrington know something? Will counted the rows of fours and guessed there were nearly one hundred cavalry soldiers.

He was feeling gloomy. What was wrong with Dove? It was bad enough to be stuck in this fort with hundreds of hostile Sioux around, but being in the company of a moody, silent woman was driving him crazy.

He loved her, but he couldn't just pretend they were married . . . could he? But did Adam and Eve have a preacher and a marriage ceremony? Or Isaac and Rebekah? Things were different now, weren't they? His heart tugged him one way, his head another. Or maybe it wasn't his heart, just lust. If he lived to be a hundred, he'd never understand women.

He decided to go past the bakery, around to the side gate. He resolved in his mind to find other diversions for the winter. Maybe he could scout or learn leatherwork if hides were available. He rounded the corner of the sutler's near the front wall of the fort and heard a woman crying.

Will hesitated. Should he intrude? Women were trouble. Common sense told him to turn around and go the other way. But he couldn't just leave someone in distress, could he?

He took two steps forward and saw a woman sitting on a log behind the store, head buried in her arms, sobbing. She looked up at his approach. It was Delilah Simmons.

Will felt awkward but gallantly said, "Miss Simmons? I'm sorry to intrude, but it sounded as though you were in distress. May I help in some way?"

Her sobs faded. "You've caught me at a disadvantage, Mr. Crump. I'm afraid I'm not very presentable. You're right; I have some distress. I'm at my wit's end and would love talking to someone. Would you mind?"

"Of course, if I may be of some service . . ."

"Oh, you can! You can! I was sitting here, feeling a bit sorry for myself, thinking I hadn't a friend in the world. And then you came. You see, I'm all alone in the world. I was married, but my husband was a drunkard and a gambler. Carson Blanchard was his name. He spent everything we had on his pleasures . . . even other women. I . . . I thought that if we could go west, get a fresh start, maybe things would get better. Then the Indian attack came, and he took an arrow through the neck. Here I am in this stupid fort, surrounded by savages. My money, the little that I have, is running out. I'm only halfway to Oregon, though what I shall do when I get there, I don't know." She sobbed again.

Will dug in his pocket and offered her a clean handkerchief. Perhaps he'd misjudged her. He felt ashamed. She was just a woman alone in a wild country, looking for a new start. And wasn't he looking for peace and a fresh beginning? A little voice in his head reminded him of what he'd just been thinking about women, but he wasn't getting involved here, just being a listening ear.

"Mrs. Blanchard . . ."

"Oh, please don't call me that. I know it's convention. I ought to be mourning my husband. But I'm not. Heaven knows he didn't treat me well. I have scars to prove it."

"All right, Miss Simmons, then. I wish I could help. But I have nothing, just my horse, my guns, a bedroll, and a tent. Surely the army—"

"The army will do exactly nothing, except perhaps send me back as far as Leavenworth. I've been there. There's nothing for me."

"And in Oregon?"

"Land. I'm not afraid of hard work. If only I had a man to file the claim for me. Not being married, I can't file anymore." She looked at Will, pleading with her eyes.

"Would you? Would you come to Oregon and file for me?"

"You mean . . . marry you ?"

"Well, yes, but only in the legal sense. Once I have the claim, you could go wherever you want. I'm strong. I know how to ride, how to plow. If I were married, I could file in my name. When you disappeared, I could say you died. Please?"

"Ma'am . . . I hardly know you. I could never do that. It would make a mockery of marriage."

She jumped up from the log and came to him, embracing him. "Then I'd be a real wife to you. I'd do anything . . . You'd grow to love me. At least say you'll think about it. No one can leave until the savages are dealt with."

She was still clinging to him when the bugle blew, sounding Boots and Saddles, and someone came around the corner . . . Clarissa. She dropped the basket in surprise at seeing Will and the woman locked in an embrace.

Dove went outside to see why the bugle blew. Just as she got past the cavalry stables, the front gate opened, and wagons came in—wagons piled with dead soldiers. Many had been scalped and mutilated: throats slit, eyes gouged out, noses cut off, limbs amputated. The Sioux made sure the white men would enter the spirit world blind and helpless. Wails of the widows rose from around the compound.

Dove noticed Will, Clarissa, and the white woman coming onto the parade ground from behind the sutler's; she wondered briefly at it, but there was too much noise to think. So much English being babbled, she could barely make out anything. A group of soldiers had gone to help the wood train, as usual, but this time they'd gone farther out. They'd gone over Lodge Trail Ridge, and the Sioux had been waiting for them. She saw Gabe and approached him, speaking in Shoshone.

"What's going on?"

"Dern fool soldiers went after a decoy group of warriors, that's what. They got themselves killed. Carrington was too scared to go after them until I told him the Sioux would be off celebrating and that they never leave their dead behind. He didn't want to be bested by some Indians, so he sent a detail back after the dead."

"Why did the stupid soldiers do that? There are thousands of Sioux and Cheyenne out there!"

"Who knows? Some were boasting they could take on the whole Sioux nation. Grummond there, especially. Now he's as full of arrows as a porcupine has quills."

"What will the soldiers do?" asked Dove.

"I don't know." He looked up at the sky. "But there's a storm coming. Even my eyes can see that. Sioux are likely going to hole up for a while. But when the storm passes . . . it could get mighty interesting here. Red Cloud ain't playing it the way they usually do. Normally they'd be miles from here, holed up in winter camp, smoking, telling stories, waiting for the thaw."

Dove furrowed her brow with worry. "Would the Sioux attack the fort?"

"Maybe. Carrington seems to think it's possible. Nothing certain, 'cept there's was more braves out there today working together than I've seen in all my days in the mountains."

Dove watched Carrington approach Will. She moved closer to hear what was said.

"Mr. Crump, you can see we are shorthanded. Phillips volunteered to ride for help. We don't know whether he'll make it, and the Indians may attack in force at any time. I need every able-bodied man in the fort. I'm afraid I can't give you much choice in this matter: either serve, or we can put you and your Indian friend in the guardhouse. I cannot be in doubt of your loyalties. Food and ammunition are scarce. If we are to feed you, you must serve."

Will considered. "All right, sir. I'll serve until you get reinforcements. But when spring comes, I'm leaving."

"Fair enough. Report to Captain Ten Eyck. You were an officer—for now, you are a brevet lieutenant in the United States Army. You may move to the officers' quarters. You'll stand guard duty. I'll assign you some of the former Confederate troops—they'll likely perform better for you than some of my other officers."

"Yes, sir."

Dove decided this suited her fine. Perhaps the colonel would let her stay in the cabin where she was, at least until the new troops came. Let Will move. He didn't seem to want to be with her anyway. Though a part of her grieved. She might have more trouble from some of the soldiers, but there was no help for it.

Will was surprised when Dove already seemed to know that he was moving and accepted it calmly. He began to think again about what she'd said, that she was capable of traveling by herself. Yet his heart wanted her, even though Will knew it was wrong. No one else would think anything of his keeping a squaw, but he would know.

He was moving the last of his things to his new quarters when he saw Clarissa and Dove.

They walked right past him as if he didn't exist. What had gotten into them?

Women! Again he resolved to pay attention to other things.

Dove invited Clarissa in and made a hot drink for both of them.

"I'm sorry, Dove," Clarissa said. "But I thought you ought to know. I would never have thought it of Will. Carrying on with another woman. But I saw them plain as day."

Dove turned toward the fire, hiding her face. "It is no matter. When the spring comes, I will return to my people. He can go with the white woman or do whatever pleases him. A woman should not be concerned with a man's choices."

Clarissa whistled in amazement. "My ma would surely pitch a fit if she heard of pa fooling with some other woman."

"There is no need. Our lodges are separated. My father never gave permission. We did not bury the hair."

Clarissa looked at her with questioning eyes.

"When two people truly join, the parents gather to give consent. A lock of hair is cut from each of their heads and braided together. They bury it somewhere near the camp. To separate, they must find it and dig it up again. Our camps move with every season. You can imagine that finding it would be difficult. But it didn't happen for us. It is the way of my people. I love Will—I don't think that is a surprise to you. If he does not wish our lodges to join together, then we should part now."

A tear escaped her eye, and she hastily wiped it away. How could she show such weakness in front of a white?

Dove continued, "If he came, there would be enough barriers to overcome. He isn't wealthy—except in guns. He has no standing with my people. It would take great determination. If he turns away at the first white woman who wants him, then he isn't who I thought he was."

The blizzard struck hard, with the wind howling in and snowdrifts two feet high. Will still went about his duties, but sometimes he felt like an icicle after guard duty. Once the storm hit, the forays of Indians close to the fort yelling war chants ceased.

Christmas came, and Will felt his loneliness keenly. He sat

and stroked Lightning, taking comfort in the soft brown eyes. Dove hadn't even visited him and avoided him on the fort grounds. What had he done now? Will missed her smile and laughter, their talks together. He wanted to sit by the fire and listen to old stories of hunts and battles from the past. He'd hoped to be able to tell her of Jesus's birth, the story in the Bible.

Each night he returned to a cold cabin, stoked up the fire from embers, and got some coffee or tea boiling. Some of the other officers invited him to drink whiskey, but he wasn't inclined.

He did some avoiding of his own, trying to stay clear of Delilah. She muddled his head, and in this weather, it was best to keep warm indoors by a fire. He only ventured out when necessary.

By New Year's, supplies in the fort were low and tempers short. The storm had passed, but the snow was knee-deep, and temperatures were still frigid. Everyone wondered what a thaw would bring.

The troop held a memorial service for the dead of the previous week's battle. No burial was possible because of the frozen ground. Will's detail provided a decent covering for them, and at present, that was the best anyone could do.

Then, late New Year's evening, an alarm sounded. The scout was now back on Pilot Hill and signaled horsemen coming.

Everyone turned out and cheered when Phillips, with two companies of cavalry and four companies of infantry, marched through the gate. They had wagons of supplies, ammunition, and mail.

Will spoke to one of the incoming soldiers.

"What's it like out there? Was it hard to travel?"

The corporal looked at him like he was slightly deranged. "Hard to travel? Yes, I guess you could say that. Snow knee- or waist-deep, twenty-five below zero. If that ain't hard, I don't want to know what is. Phillips there, his horse died as soon as he arrived—just keeled over. There was quite a debate about whether to come or wait for spring. But Phillips made it sound desperate. So here we are. All I want is a warm fire and to sleep for a week."

Will walked over to the sutler's, thinking to get warm by the stove. As he extended his frozen hands toward the fire grate, he heard soldiers talking.

"Yep, Carrington's gone. Finally! Headquarters saw through his yellow-belly ways, not taking on the Injuns."

"You must be new; you wouldn't call him yellow if you'd seen the fight last week. He let those have their way that thought they could whip the Sioux with their hands tied. And he went out with the troop that tried to rescue Fetterman, hoping for some still alive, but not a single man survived."

"Well, anyhow, he's recalled. I don't envy him the march back to Laramie. We all nigh froze to death."

"Yes, and he'll have women and children as if the weather wasn't enough. That's the army for you."

After Will warmed himself and had some coffee, he asked the sutler if any mail had come on the wagon for him. The storekeeper rooted around a bit and said, "Ah, yes. Crump. It looks like old news, forwarded from Leavenworth and Laramie. Here you go!"

Will took the battered letter, immediately recognizing Albinia's writing. Opening it, he scanned it, planning to read it in more detail in his quarters. Albinia and Peter had a baby boy, Charles. Julia had suffered a miscarriage. Luther, Sam, and Ruth, their black friends, had been driven out of Indiana and settled in Kansas. Ma and Pa were doing well, with Pa having started his dry-goods store. Will marveled at how much had happened, but he felt guilty that he had not written home more. He'd have to fix that if the weather ever broke.

He emerged from the store onto the parade ground to see Dove trudging across it, carrying a heavy load, going toward the stable. He hurried toward her, the wind howling around them.

"Dove! Dove! Wait! What are you doing?"

"There are new men, a new commander. He says cabins are not for squaws. I'm going to the stables until I can build a lodge of my own."

"In this cold? You can't! You'll freeze to death."

"And if I did, what concern is that of yours? I lived through many winters in what you call a tipi with a fire. All my life, I've lived outdoors. So if I don't survive, it's because I've become soft, like a white woman."

"Dove, let me help you. Please. Come and stay with me again. You'll be warm. We'll work things out."

"What is there to work out? Don't you have your golden-haired woman? Is she not in your cabin already? I am not your slave, and I have no desire to be a second wife."

"What do you mean? I have no golden-haired woman! There's no one in the cabin with me—come and see for yourself."

"You're just like the other white men! Lies! I thought you were different. I should have known. When did you plan to tell me? As I got ready to leave for my people? Clarissa saw you and the woman together. Good-bye, Will!"

Dove strode off toward the stables, her blankets trailing behind her. Will stared after her, too stunned to move.

CHAPTER ELEVEN

Dove threw her things down in the corner of the stable. She gathered some firewood from the post stores—surely they wouldn't begrudge her that! Picking an area of bare ground where the stable walls gave some protection from the wind, Dove worked to get a fire going using her fire drill. It took patience, and her hands were numb by the time she got a good blaze going. She'd need to stretch some skins over a frame for shelter.

Why did I believe him? Men care only for their pleasures; why should Will be different? She slammed her ax into the wood. It felt good. She hoped the yellow hair ended up on a lance, though there would be no honor in scalping a woman. How she missed her lodge among her people! Her father wanted her to marry Kajika, his cousin's nephew, but she had rejected him. Why? He was a brave warrior, owned many horses, and was respected among the men.

She split another piece of wood in one stroke, pounding it in her anger. What was she doing here, following a white man? She should have been safe in her lodge. Washakie would not have refused to look after her, even if her father did not welcome her.

Still, she did have to admit that Will had risked himself to save her from the Cheyenne. He didn't have to do that; he could have just gone back to the fort in safety. She thought of the tender moments, the kisses they'd shared. And he had proved her innocent in the trial when the soldiers would have hanged her.

She shook her head, angry at herself. What was the good in wallowing in what was past?

Kaihinasumbanrayde daingwa! Stupid man! Why did she care about him?

Will sat on his bunk, watching the fire in the fireplace. His gloomy thoughts were interrupted by a knock at the door. Hopeful, he withdrew the string latch and opened it.

"May I come in?" Clarissa said.

"Sure, Clarissa." Once she was out of the cold, he asked, "What can I do for you?"

"Not much. It's more about what you've done to Dove. She's my friend. I thought she was yours too."

Will wrinkled his brow, staring at her. "What do you mean?"

"I mean, I saw you with that blond woman when the wagons came back with all the dead soldiers. I couldn't believe it, but there you were, holding her. Maybe I'm not safe here myself! But I felt like someone had to confront you. You've hurt Dove like an arrow to the gut. How could you do that after all the two of you have been through together? I thought you were an honorable man."

Will stood. His tone was sharp.

"Now just a minute! You're in over your head here, young lady. If it's any of your business, I went over to the store and the bakery. As I left, I heard a woman crying. I thought maybe I could help. It was Miss Simmons, the blond lady you saw. She was very distraught. Before I knew what was happening, she jumped into my arms, saying she wanted me to marry her! Then you came along. I hardly had a chance to respond."

Clarissa glared at him. "And what were you going to say? Your response looked pretty clear to me."

"Dove and I have been having . . . misunderstandings. This woman wanted me to be her partner, follow her to Oregon so she could get land. Of course, it's impossible. I need to find a polite way to tell her no without hurting her feelings. I always have a soft spot for helping folks in trouble, but I think this one is just more than I can handle. I prayed about it, and I don't think it's my problem. But it sure enough made things worse with Dove, I guess. Is that why she's all upset? Because you told her?"

"Well, what would you expect me to do?" Clarissa said defensively. "It would hurt her worse to let you deceive her."

"Why don't you sit and have some tea?" Will indicated the rude chairs and a table made from barrels and a board.

Clarissa sat reluctantly. He handed her a steaming cup of tea.

"Nobody's deceiving anybody here, 'cept maybe you deceiving yourself. I barely know Miss Simmons. I'm sorry for her losing her husband, but that happens to women moving west—I can't help them all. I admit I felt confused for a bit because of our troubles. But I promised to help Dove. I promised to see her home safe. I don't take that lightly. I do love her. I don't know how things will turn out between us. I will honor her choice."

Clarissa looked doubtful. "So you're saying she just jumped into your arms without really knowing you? And proposed marriage?"

"That's about the size of it. It's the truth, whether you believe me or not."

"Why would she do a thing like that?"

"Best I can figure, she'd do anything to be able to claim land in Oregon. She can't do it alone, so . . ."

"I guess that makes sense. When are you going to tell Miss Simmons?"

"Tonight, if I can. I'm on guard duty, at the main gate. Maybe you and your ma could find Miss Simmons, bring her to the gate so I have witnesses. Six o'clock watch, just after dark."

"Are you sure?"

"No telling what she might try if nobody's around. I'm in enough trouble as it is."

"All right. I'll tell Ma."

Will pulled out the deer horn he'd been working on, hollowing it out, trying to make a gift for Dove. It was probably pointless given the state of their relationship, but just in case, he wanted to be ready if she would receive it.

He'd just completed a pair of buffalo boots. Mrs. Grummond had shown him how to make them before she left. He didn't tell her they were for Dove, and she had assumed they were for one of the other women in the fort.

Another knock at the door interrupted his work.

When he opened it, he found Gabe.

"Got time for an old feller?"

"Sure, Gabe. Come in. Have a pipe and some coffee. The company would be good."

Gabe shuffled in, chuckling. "Getting things patched up with Dove?"

"Not really. It's still pretty bleak."

"You need to show her she's more important to you than anyone else. A few gifts like them boots wouldn't hurt. Bring her food. The army won't give her much. Don't take no for an answer— keep after her. She can't go anywhere for a while yet."

"You think so?"

"If a woman hates you, not much gonna change her mind. If she's feeling neglected and jealous but cares about you, attention and keeping after her are likely gonna bring a spring thaw."

Will's spirits lifted.

Will climbed the steps to the gate at the bridge across the Platte at sunset. The cold was bothering his ankle. It stung when he put weight on it. The ground glistened with ice and snow. He had a feeling his nose was going to freeze off before this shift was over. It had never been this cold in Tennessee or Kentucky during the war. It reminded him of shivering times in Camp Douglas, near Chicago, when he had been a prisoner of war. Unlike the camp, no one here had come down with smallpox, dysentery, or the grippe.

He stared out into the waning light as the sun dipped behind Lodge Trail Ridge. How did Gabe ever do it? The old man's eyes were failing now, but Will knew he would have seen where the Sioux scouts were in his prime. Will could make out a wisp of smoke above the trees to the northwest. It could be a Sioux camp, but Will had no notion of how large. He walked up and down, carrying his rifle on his shoulder, glancing up occasionally to the east to see if the scout on Pilot Hill was still there.

As the last rays faded, he heard his name.

"Will! We've come. We couldn't find Miss Simmons anywhere, though. She couldn't have left the fort, but none of the women have seen her."

"Clarissa! Mrs. Cochran! Thank you for coming. I can't imagine where she could have gone. Did you check the sutler? She seems to hang around there sometimes."

"Yes, we peeked in. He's about to close for the night—no Miss Simmons."

"Corporal!"

A soldier came running. "Yes, sir!"

"Can you spell me for a few minutes here while I assist these ladies?"

"Yes, sir!"

Will gave the duty to the corporal. Before leaving, he peered into the dimness in the interior of the fort, looking for any movement against the white background of the snow. A few men moved on the parade ground and over by the teamsters' quarters, but otherwise, it seemed still.

Then over behind the company quarters, he saw a flash, like something reflecting off metal.

"Let's go see what's up over there," said Will.

Clarissa and Mrs. Cochran dutifully followed him. As they drew closer, they heard sounds, then voices.

"Oh, please, please! Yes!" a woman's voice said, followed by a man's guttural growl.

As they rounded the corner, Mrs. Cochran exclaimed, "Well, I never!" and covered Clarissa's eyes.

Far from being in distress, it appeared the woman, Miss Simmons, Will now recognized, was in the throes of pleasure, up against a wall with a private, not quite in uniform, holding her up. They seemed oblivious to the cold—and the newcomers.

Will turned away. "Come, ladies. I'm sorry to have troubled you. It appears this woman has all the assistance she needs."

When he rose the next morning while it was still dark, he dressed and took the buffalo boots and a beautiful buffalo robe over to Dove's campsite, along with a haunch from a deer that had ventured too close to the fort. She was sleeping, but he knew her watchfulness would be on a hair-trigger amid all these soldiers, so he moved as quietly as Gabe had taught him. He didn't dare lay the robe over her. She'd probably spring to her feet, knife in hand, ready to cut the throat of her attacker. He laid the gifts behind her, near the stable wall, and built up the fire a little. He debated whether to stay or go. He sat quietly by the fire and waited. As the sun peeked over Pilot Hill, the temperature warmed almost to freezing.

Dove stretched, yawned, and became aware of someone else there. She jumped, then tensed as she realized it was Will.

"What are you doing here?"

"I came to see you. I miss you."

She made a doubtful noise in her throat. "More likely, you came to see your horse."

Just then, Clarissa arrived.

"Well, it seems I am to have no peace to pray and greet the sun this morning."

"Oh, Dove, don't be cross," Clarissa said. She smiled at Will. "I thought I heard a call for reinforcements."

"That you did!" Will grinned.

Clarissa turned to Dove. "I want to apologize to both of you. I made assumptions. I gossiped. And I caused trouble where there shouldn't have been any. That horrible woman! Dove, Will is telling the truth. She was using him. I . . . I saw what no decent woman should have to see. She's nothing more than a common whore."

"What is . . . whore?"

"A woman who sells herself for money. I asked Gabe. You call it *noyokowa'ippü*."

"Ah. A woman would only do that if she is poor and ugly or diseased, and no man wants her in his lodge, even as a slave."

"Anyway, I just wanted to say how sorry I am for causing trouble. I'll leave you two to talk."

As Clarissa moved away, Will stammered, "Dove, I—I don't know what to say. I want you to know that I love you. I never had anything to do with Miss Simmons. If you don't believe me, at least believe Clarissa. Mrs. Cochran saw it too. I promised to see you to your people. I intend to keep that promise if you'll let me."

"But you don't love me. You don't want me."

"How can I explain? I do want you so much. You've been in my dreams. I know you put store by dreams. I've dreamed of you, of your people, of holding you in my arms. But my Great Father, my God, wants the joining of man and woman to be sacred and forever. Many whites do not follow Him or His book, but I do. When I see you, I am *na'isape*; my heart is on fire. But I must not do this thing."

"Why not? It is normal for a man and a woman to want each other."

"Yes, but my God in His book says that both the man and the woman must be His followers, his children, or neither. It won't work to have one a follower and one not. And there must be a marriage, a promise."

"Yes, I've seen these things, from the Black Robes that come among us. They tell us we are bad that we do wrong. We must become like whites. The whites from the Lake of Salt tell us their way is right—but they have many wives, which the Black Robes say is wrong. Other white men do not care about the Father, the Great Mystery. They do as they please. White men are confusing."

Will sighed. Explaining wasn't getting him anywhere. "The answers are in God's book, the Bible, no matter what anyone says. For now, I can't take you to my bed, but I love you. Today is a holiday for lovers among my people. It's called Valentine's Day. Look behind you."

Dove turned and saw the boots, the robe, and the deer. "You have been a hunter for me?" A smile tugged at the edge of her lips as she softened.

"I just brought you a few gifts. If you're going to stay here, you should at least be warm. But I have walls and fire. You are welcome back in the cabin, as we were before."

He rose and came around the fire.

"Will you come?"

She rose and began gathering her things. They kicked snow on the fire and walked to the cabin together.

The weather turned bitter cold. Will rubbed his hands together, getting the blood going. The commander wasn't calling on him for watches as often because the Sioux didn't venture close to the fort. But he was still cautious and kept a few horses saddled and ready. The fort froze in time, a winter landscape painting of frosted trees, snow piled like haystacks, and needles of ice, where nothing moved but the ceaseless wind.

Will stomped the snow off his feet as he entered the cabin and laid down the sutler's supplies. The aroma from the stove pulled at his hunger, and he went over to wrap his arms around Dove. She smiled but pushed him away. "Aren't you hungry?"

"Yes," he admitted. "But just as hungry for you."

Dove served venison stew for both of them and then pulled him into her Valentine's buffalo robe. Will marveled at the sheen of the firelight on her hair. Her arm circled him, and he leaned back against her.

Will stared thoughtfully at the fire. "I want to learn more about your people, their stories and customs, to help me understand you better. Fire is important, right? How do the Shoshone say the earth started?"

"It seems a good night for stories," Dove began. "Our Father, the Great Mystery, made the earth, and he was walking on it with his wife and son. The earth caught on fire. They walked among the flames, but Father cautioned them not to look back at the fire. The fire roared in among them, threatening to catch their skirts on fire. The woman felt it and was afraid. She looked back and was instantly turned to stone because she had done what Father told her not to do. Father had a walking stick, which he put to the ground in front of them. He and his son walked on. Wherever the stick touched, the blaze went out. Behind the fire came the water, covering the earth. Soon the flames were out. Father made himself and his son small so that they could ride the foam of the waves. Father thought about how to get the earth back again. First, he made himself and his son one being. They remained there as Father called the water creatures until he found one who could dive deep enough to get to the bottom. Otter volunteered after Beaver and Muskrat failed.

"They waited a long time. Father was about to give up when they saw Otter's body floating to the top. It was bloated with water—he had drowned. Father pulled Otter on top of the foam and made him come to life again. As Muskrat helped Father, they discovered mud under Muskrat's nails.

"Father said, 'You did find Earth.'

"Father took the mud, rolled it into a ball, and then flattened it out. He rolled it, flattened it, over and over, each time growing a little larger. When it was big enough, he laid the flattened earth over the top of the water.

"He made hills and mountains, springs and rivers, trees and flowers. Then he made different kinds of birds and animals. When Father was satisfied, he made the earth turn. With the earth facing the sun, it was spring and summer. If the sun hid in the gray and dark, it was winter."

Will pulled her on top of him, tucked into the buffalo robe, and put his arms around her.

"That's not so different from my people's story. After we eat, I'll read ours to you from the Bible."

He kissed her. She answered, tentatively at first, then parted her lips and responded with more passion.

"The stew will get cold," he said.

"I don't care if you don't." She wiggled closer.

He kissed her twice more, clutched her tighter, and then with effort said, "Maybe . . . maybe I'd better care. The stew may get cold, but much more of that, and I'll be on fire."

She smiled at him mischievously. "And what's wrong with that?"

"Hmm," Will said, grabbing his stew and the Bible, moving to the table. They ate while he read. "In the beginning, God created the heavens and the earth . . ."

She seemed to listen, but after she finished her stew, she moved to the robes and shut her eyes.

He droned on a while but realized after a few minutes that she was warm and full. She had fallen asleep.

CHAPTER TWELVE

Will inspected their gear and rations. Gabe had promised to go with them, to see his friend Washakie, and then go to his daughter in St. Louis. Dove tended to most of the packing.

"Don't know how much help I'm gonna be to you, 'cept talking to Washakie. Can't see more'n forty feet. Durndest thing—used to could see miles and miles. I can listen, and I can smell. But you'd better rely on that gal o' yours for any warning of trouble."

"We'll do all right as long as we stay clear of Sioux war parties and Cheyenne dog soldiers."

"Colonel give you his release?"

"Yeah, I think he's glad to see the back of me, especially if it means getting Dove out of his fort."

"Do you know where you're going?"

The thought struck Will like a thunderclap.

"I just assumed you or Dove would know."

"Where to find Washakie?" Gabe snorted. "You're still a greenhorn, ain'tcha? Bands move around. It ain't like walking up to an address in St. Louis and knocking on the door. It depends on what kind of fall and winter they had, where the buffalo are going, how the weather has been. They'll follow the buffalo; that's about all you can be sure of."

Dove said, "The buffalo have been moving north lately, to get away from the whites. We are already close to Crow country, and there are still Sioux and Cheyenne. We should go south, maybe toward Fort Bridger. If we do not see them or get news of them, the traders in the fort will know what their plans are."

Gabe rubbed his chin. "That makes a lot of sense, little lady."

Will considered. "Then that's where we'll head. If there are soldiers, there's less likely to be large war parties, seems to me."

"Not necessarily. But I can guide you there, even if I was stone blind."

"Fair enough. Let's get started." Will looked at the sky to the northeast, seeing thunderclouds. "I don't much like the look of the weather. Looks like a storm coming."

"Might be a wet night," Gabe agreed.

Dove mounted her pony and took the lead, followed by Will and Lightning, with Gabe bringing up the rear. Gabe figured he could hear trouble from behind while Dove would recognize landmarks, and Will would be able to help either one in case of attack.

The little party trotted through the gates of Fort Phil Kearny. The Sioux had not attacked the wood trains yet. They figured it was a good time to go before the Sioux hunted buffalo and whites on the trail. Will cast a nervous glance back at the lookout on Pilot Hill but saw nothing unusual—except forks of lightning in the east.

They headed southeast at first, detouring around Cloud Peak and the Bighorns.

The rain held off for an hour or so, then started gently. They made good time. The game in the area had holed up in anticipation of a storm. Their little party made about sixteen miles, traveling along Lake De Smet and down to Clear Creek.

The wind began to pick up.

Gabe called ahead.

"Don't like the look of the weather! Better camp here, get a fire going while we can. Nothing's going to move until the storm is over."

Dove looked up. "You're right, Gabe. Time to stop."

They tied their horses to cottonwood trees near the creek and quickly set up a tent for each of them. Will improvised a canvas tarp over a small area in the center of the tents, and Dove got a fire going. Lightning found a dry spot under a rock overhang, turned several times, and settled.

They'd barely completed their preparations when the rain began falling in sheets, drenching everything. The wind howled, making it hard to talk.

Will had just climbed into his bedroll to stay warm when he saw moccasins at the door of the tent.

"I'm cold!" Dove yelled.

"Come in out of the wet, then," said Will irritably. Didn't she have her tent? After all, they hadn't been sharing a bed at the fort.

After he re-tied the tent flap and offered her his blanket, she snuggled in next to him.

"Better?"

"Yes, this is much better. Next time you can save yourself the trouble and just set up one tent, keep the other dry. We can trade tents back and forth," Dove said practically.

"I suppose that makes sense."

"Of course it does. And if Sioux attack at night, we'll both know at once. Lightning will bark. Gabe is standing watch over the horses until he gets tired."

"And you're standing watch over me, is that it?"

"Exactly!" she giggled. "White men like you need watching."

"Hmpf. I think Shoshone women like you need watching."

"Oh! I hope you'll watch me all night."

Her hand reached over and explored his chest, untying the laces at the neck of his buckskin shirt.

"We'd better think of another less dangerous occupation," he said, gently removing her hand.

Morning came, and the chinook blew, warming the temperatures. She was up with the sun, making a fire and coffee that the white men liked. She'd learned that Will was much happier after some peace and morning coffee. Their breakfast was simple and brief. They struck camp and started on the trail again.

Dove kept alert for signs of animals, enemies, or any tracks that might indicate the passing of her people. It wasn't likely they would find them before reaching Fort Bridger, but anything was possible. She didn't know for sure where the band might have wintered or where the buffalo were this spring.

The warmer temperatures were causing the snow to melt at higher elevations. The trail was a muddy mess and turned sharply upward as they reached the entrance to Crazy Woman Canyon, or so she'd learned the whites called it. She glanced back at Will. He seemed to be trusting in her ability to guide them. Gabe kept pace, smoking on a cheroot as he rode.

Here and there, she saw signs of deer or elk, and smaller animals scurried out of the way of Lightning and the horses, but she saw no evidence of humans passing recently. They continued down the western slope of the ridge on the game trail, winding around boulders and rock walls until reaching the bottom at Crazy Woman Creek. The creek gushed with snowmelt but was small enough to cross without difficulty.

She turned them west, and toward evening they came to the Bighorn River. She wasn't feeling well. She felt bloated and sore. Her abdomen ached, and she suspected her monthlies were starting. She said several choice curse words in Shoshone. Why now?

"Will, I've changed my mind. Please set up a separate tent for me tonight. It looks like it will be a good night, and I want to sleep well. We're going to have to cross this river tomorrow."

"Whatever you want, Dove."

She looked at the river in some dismay. Usually, it was wide, but not deep. She'd never crossed it except in late summer. Now the river was a raging torrent, crashing along and pulling with it everything in its path.

Gabe came up beside her.

"If that river is anything like what I'm hearing, we're gonna have to think some on how to cross it."

As they approached the river the next day, Will stared at the frothing foam tumbling over boulders, moving faster than a trotter.

"What do you think is the best way across?" Will asked Gabe.

"Well, I've got some ropes and a pulley. Two of us could go over with our horses, the third stay back, run the pulley to get powder, shot, and supplies across, then come with the last horse. That water is purty near freezing, and we have no idea how deep it gets. See all them boulders? Horse or man smash into one of them, and we'll be in a fine mess."

"Or," said Dove, "we could look for another place downstream where it's quieter and easier to cross."

Gabe shook his head. "I recollect farther downstream the mountains get higher, and the river goes through some canyons with no way across. I doubt we'd do better."

"All right, we'll do it Gabe's way," said Will. "Who goes across first? I'm probably the strongest, Gabe the most experienced, and Dove the lightest."

Gabe said, "I'll take the rope across, tied to my saddle. Think you can set up the pulley, Will?"

"Sure."

"Smear everything you can with bear grease to keep it dry. Got some in that pouch on my horse," Gabe said, pointing.

Gabe showed Will how to package up his powder and shot to go across on the rope, then went to the bank, leading his horse, and waded in. He hung on to the saddle and braced against boulders but then came to a stretch where there was nothing but open water until the far bank. The water was chest-deep at that point, the other bank about fifty feet away. Gabe urged the horse forward, swimming as hard as he could. His head disappeared below the water. Will's heart slammed in his chest with worry for the old man—could he make it?

Within a few minutes, the horse began to clamber up the opposite bank, about a hundred feet downstream. And there was Gabe, coughing and sputtering but trudging up the other side. He waved at the top of the bank and led his horse back to the point across from them. He tied the rope securely around a low point on a tree so that it angled down across the river. The second rope would bind to the pulley to pull it back across the stream to Will after delivering their parcel to the other side.

Gabe worked on building a fire to dry their clothing, and it was Dove's turn. She bundled up her belongings in deerskin and, climbing up on a large boulder, attached it to the waiting pulley. As she let go, the parcel rolled across the raging river, still a foot above the water at the lowest point. The bundle had her knife and her bow and arrows along with a spare dress and her fire drill.

Will watched her go down to the water. Lightning paced the riverbank, whining.

Dove stood at the water's edge, fighting nausea. She wished they could wait a few days until she felt better. Holding on to her pony's mane, she urged her forward into the water. The pony trusted her and stayed with her, wide eyes showing whites the only sign of fear. The river was up to her thighs. The cold numbed her. The current caused her to stumble, jagged rocks tearing at her bare feet.

A muscle cramp hit in her abdomen. She lost her grip on the pony. She floundered forward after her, falling face-first into the water. When she came up spluttering, she saw the pony shy away from an arrow that landed in the water a foot away. Gabe was grappling with an Indian on the shore. She tried to regain her feet, then thought better of it and went under the water to avoid arrows. Her pony thrashed wildly and moved farther away. She started swimming underwater, hoping she didn't smash into a boulder or come up right in front of her enemies with no weapons. Another cramp hit. She wanted to cry out but needed to save her air. She kicked and briefly brought her head above water, gulping air. She turned and saw Will diving into the water, followed by Lightning, to rescue her.

She couldn't help him. She had to get to the other side, help Gabe. She struck out, determined, kicking, swimming parallel with the current, moving ever so slightly toward Gabe's bank with each stroke, dodging boulders until she couldn't avoid them fast enough, and one grazed her head.

Dove fought for consciousness. Her hands touched gravelly sand. She pulled herself forward, out of the water, kneeling on the shore. She looked around, ready to fight, but didn't see anyone.

She crouched low behind some bushes and listened carefully. She only heard the roar of the water. She was aching, bruised, and tired. But what had happened to Will and Gabe? This was no time to sit and rest, as she longed to do.

She poked her head up again and looked carefully in all directions. She thought she saw Will's horse, across the river and back upstream. She worked her way farther up onto the bank, found a game trail, and followed it upstream, watching all around her. She saw moccasin prints on the trail, but the brush was thick, and the bank was steep. She'd risk falling into the river if she detoured on that side. What if Gabe or Will was hurt and needed help quickly? But what if they were captive . . . or dead? She had no weapons, no horse—what could a woman alone do against warriors?

Still going carefully, she saw the clearing ahead where Gabe had been and the rope stretching across the river. And there lay Gabe, apparently unconscious, with two Crow warriors, one on either side. She was sure they were dead because one had an iron hatchet lodged in his skull, and the other had a large knife buried to the hilt in the heart area. Gabe's horse was still tethered there, along with his and her belongings.

She quickly armed herself, grabbing knife and bow, then bent over Gabe. He had a gash on his head, but he was breathing. She saw a war club off to the side, caked with blood.

Where was Will? Alone, she couldn't hope to rescue him from a war party. And she had a patient, a dear friend of Washakie, right in front of her.

She grabbed a cup, went to the river, and washed the wound on the back of Gabe's head, lifting it gently. He groaned, then let loose a stream of English swear words she couldn't follow. She caught "cussed Crow" a few times. The wound seemed mostly superficial, as though the war club had glanced off his head as he rolled to the side.

What to do? They couldn't stay here long, but Gabe couldn't move. She needed to find Will or at least evidence of what had happened to him. What if the Crow returned?

She asked Gabe in Shoshone, "Where are you hurt? Just your head or other wounds?"

"Just my head. I'll be all right if you put that repeating rifle where I can reach it. Where's Will?"

"I don't know. I think he dived into the river to save me, but there's no sign of him. His horse is still there, so I don't think the Crow are on the other side. I can see his rifle in the saddle scabbard—they'd never leave a horse and a fine rifle behind. He may have washed downstream. I don't think he's a swimmer."

"Take a pistol. Go down the river, cautious like, and look for Will. If you aren't back by morning, I'll try to follow it. I'd offer my horse, but you'll attract less attention on foot. Where's your pony?"

"I don't know. I think the Crow got her."

Dove made sure Gabe had water and hardtack near at hand, along with a box of shells for the rifle. She used a leather thong to tie the pistol around her neck, leaving her hands free. She had her knife, bow and arrows, and a small amount of hardtack for herself. Not her favorite food, but the white man's food would keep her from starving. There was no telling how far downstream Will might be or his condition.

Her worst fear was running into the Crow or having them return, maybe with reinforcements. One Shoshone pony wasn't much plunder. How many were there? She didn't know that either.

She traveled on the game trail, exhausted, hurting, bleeding from her monthlies. It just wasn't fair.

Sometimes the brush was too high to see over, and she had to stop and fight her way through to the river edge lest she miss Will washed up on a bank. She saw horse tracks—this must be where the Crow had kept their horses while the attack was going on. What if there were horses still around, the ones the fallen warriors had ridden?

The trail went down slightly before heading sharply up. Dove figured she must be nearing the canyons, with sheer walls on both sides of the river. At the low point, there was a clearing, and she saw two horses grazing with no apparent guard. Maybe Gabe had killed them all? Maybe two was all there were?

Their heads went up at her approach. She whispered to them. They each had a sort of rough rope bridle and no saddle. There was a dappled Appaloosa, and a roan-colored quarter horse stamped with a US brand on the rump. The Crow must have stolen them from soldiers. She approached the roan, getting close enough to stroke its neck. Dove grabbed the bridle, careful not to move too suddenly.

She kept stroking the neck and then moved toward the Appaloosa. It nervously shied away. She patiently moved closer again, and it reared, wheeled, and ran. The other horse jerked as if to follow its companion but yielded to the bridle. Her hand got rope burn from hanging on, but she wasn't dragged and did not release it.

She continued to stroke and talked soothingly to the roan, and after a minute or two, it was willing to be led. Now at least if she found Will hurt, she'd have a way to get him back to Gabe.

Dove walked out of the clearing, one hand on the bridle, the other on her knife, still looking carefully and checking for tracks. She saw horse tracks coming into the clearing but none leaving, giving her further confidence that there had only been two Crow warriors who had thought them easy prey.

The trail turned sharply up, but just before entering a canyon, she saw a horse tethered and loose rocks scattered as though someone had made their way down. She looked below and saw an Indian bent over a man lying facedown next to the river. Will!

The Indian didn't look like Crow and didn't seem to be aware of her presence, but she was cautious. She made her way down but knocked rocks and pebbles before her, causing the Indian to whirl and aim a bow in her direction. Seeing a woman, he lowered it.

With no further threat, she had to concentrate on the slope to avoid falling. When Dove reached the bottom, she saw Will, apparently unconscious on the bank, and bending over him was Kajika, her erstwhile suitor.

She was shocked and confused. Joy at seeing Will alive, as his chest moved up and down, happy to see someone from her tribe, but did it have to be Kajika?

"Dove! Why are you here?"

"I am traveling to our people with this white man and Old Gabe."

Just then, Will's eyes fluttered open, turning toward the sound of her voice.

"Dove!" He tried to sit up and fell back.

Kajika said, "This man knows you—who is he?"

"He is called Will Crump. I can tell you about him."

"Later. For now, we must get him to a place of safety."

"Old Gabe is also hurt. Two Crow attacked us while crossing the river. Will's horse and gear are back upstream, along with Gabe. I can make a stretcher if he can't walk."

"Stop talking about me like I'm dead. I hear, and I'll be all right. Some bumps and bruises, a little too much water, and a bad headache." He rolled to his side, pulled a leg up, and pushed up to a kneeling position.

"Do you think you can walk?"

"In a few minutes, yes. How badly is Gabe hurt?"

"A knock on the head from a Crow war club. But he killed them both."

"And you?"

"Wet, cold, and sore. And hungry. But otherwise, all right. What happened?"

"I saw those Crow shooting at you, your pony went crazy, and then you disappeared. I jumped in to save you and slammed against a boulder. I tried to swim and keep my head above water. I guess I passed out. I woke up here. Did they get Dusty?"

"No, your horse and your rifle were safe when I came to find you. But I don't know for how long. I haven't seen Lightning anywhere."

"Let's go, then. Sir, can you give me a hand?"

Kajika reached out and helped Will to stand. He and Kajika worked together, and after about half an hour, they reached the top of the slope. They helped Will mount the roan behind Dove, who began guiding them back to Gabe.

When they arrived, Gabe had rekindled the fire and was sitting on a stump. The sun still peeked over the mountains in a ball of fiery orange.

Dove made introductions. "Will, this is Kajika. He is from my village."

"Does he speak English?"

"Not much."

Will tried his Shoshone, with Gabe and Dove giving encouraging smiles.

"Thank you. You found me just in time."

Kajika gave a quick nod and turned away.

They set up camp there. Will watched Kajika jump into the river. With sure, strong strokes, he swam across and got Dusty and all of Will's gear. He didn't even seem tired and shook off the water like a dog. Will saw muscles ripple in his arms and chest and was glad Kajika was Dove's friend and not an enemy. He sat and wrapped himself in a buffalo robe for warmth for a few minutes, then walked into the darkness.

Will began to worry about Lightning but lacked the strength to go looking for him. Just as he was about to say something about it to Dove, the wet, bedraggled mutt came up from the riverbank, trotting and panting, flopping down next to Will and the fire.

Kajika returned in half an hour with a few rabbits, which Dove skinned and roasted. It wasn't much for three men and a woman, but it was better than nothing. Gabe produced a pipe, filled it with tobacco, and passed it to Kajika. Dove was uncharacteristically quiet. Will stayed wrapped in a robe, moving as little as possible. When the pipe came to him, he wanted to decline but caught the signal from Dove that he must accept. He pulled a drought and coughed. He wasn't used to tobacco.

After a few more puffs, Will no longer coughed and gagged as much, but privately he vowed never to make it a habit.

Dove did not join them at the fire but stayed in the background. Will wondered at the curious transformation. Was it Kajika that was making her act differently?

After dinner, when the pipe bowl began to empty, Gabe asked Kajika, "Where are Washakie and his band?"

"Six sleeps south. I came to scout north for buffalo. We have not seen herds yet this spring, and the people are hungry."

"We can rest here a day or two, as long as the Crow don't come back. Seems those two," he gestured to the covered bodies of the warriors, "were traveling alone, so they won't be missed for some time."

Dove helped set up the tents and made Kajika a temporary lodge of saplings and stretched hide. She carried water and wood for the fires. She felt better physically, but Kajika worried her. How would Kajika react to Will, especially once he suspected her feelings?

Dove resolved to stay quiet and not give Kajika any reason for jealousy, at least until they reached Washakie's camp.

She spent the next day close to the camp, tending wounds and drying gear. Kajika had used their rope pulley and gotten everything across. She saw him look longingly at Will's rifle. She would have to warn Will. If Kajika saw him as a rival, it could be dangerous for him.

Kajika rode out to look for buffalo, coming back only at sunset. He returned with an antelope slung over his horse but no word of the buffalo.

Dove saw Will's questioning look, but she signed him with her back turned to Kajika to let her alone. She quickly made the sign for danger, causing him to stand dizzily and then sink back.

Gabe was better off than Will but still stayed close to camp for the day. His eyesight would not have helped to find the buffalo, and his head hurt. Dove saw him take a swig or two from a whiskey flask.

The next day went much the same. On the third day, Kajika came thundering back just after the sun was at its highest point.

"I've found them! A large herd. We must go back to camp and tell the other men."

"Will still cannot ride far at a time."

"Then we can leave the white men. Let Gabe nurse the sick one. This news will not wait."

"Go, then. Tell the band. Where is Washakie? We will find you as we started to do."

"The band is near the white man's trail, where some go south, others north—the place they call South Pass. Why not come with me? Gabe does not need you to play shaman."

"These are my friends. I want to go home, but I don't want to abandon them. We set out together; we will arrive together."

"I could take you. These men cannot stop me."

Dove stepped back and pulled up the revolver on the leather string around her neck to where she could grasp it, holding it loosely in the palm of her right hand. She looked Kajika in the eye, fingering it.

"Perhaps. But Will would try. And when he is well, he bites at a very long distance with that rifle."

"Then I will kill him and take the rifle as well."

She pulled the knife into view on its thong. "If you do that, I will kill you. You must sleep sometime."

"The whites have made your head soft. And what will you do if Crow or Blackfeet come? One old man and a broken, soft white?"

"We will hide. Or we will fight. Gabe is well known to you; he is not just an old man. Will rescued me from Cheyenne dog soldiers—all by himself. You should not underestimate him."

"*Ainwambe am'bo!* Foolish woman!" Kajika stomped off to his wikiup.

Will awoke with a headache but otherwise felt better. He sat up, pulled himself out of the tent, and saw that Dove and Gabe had a fire, coffee, and breakfast ready. Kajika was nowhere around.

After coffee and food, he braced on a tree and tried standing. When that was successful, he risked a few tottering steps. He didn't fall over, which he counted as a victory. He rested, then tried walking over to Dusty. He decided to keep his rifle with him and a box of cap-and-ball cartridges for the Navy Colt on his hip. Like in the war, he felt safer with it near at hand, not knowing when trouble might strike.

"How are you today?" Dove asked.

"Alive and better, thanks to all of you. I should know better than to think you needed rescuing."

"Ah . . . but sometimes I do."

"I didn't do much. It seems like you saved Gabe and me again."

"Kajika found you. I only helped carry you up to the horse and then back here. I must warn you, though, Kajika thinks you are a threat."

"A threat? Why?"

"He sees that we care for one another. Remember, he asked my parents for me as a wife. He is jealous."

She moved closer to him. "And he has reason to be." Gabe had wandered off, so she kissed him. A little at first, then more.

"Whoa!" said Will. "My head was already spinning. Take it easy on a fella."

"All right. But only until you recover. Can you ride today? Or shoot?"

"Maybe. I might be able to ride some. I could shoot, but I don't swear about hitting much. I'm still shaky."

"Kajika found buffalo. He must get word back to Washakie. We need to go soon. We've already stayed long enough that other Crow may come looking for their relatives. Also, I don't like staying so near where those warriors died. Their ghosts could return for us."

"Ghosts?"

"Each body has two spirits. When the body dies, the spirit flies free, but it may come back to the place of death and try to take others with it to the place of the dead."

Will shook his head. "That's too much for morning and one cup of coffee. But I agree we need to move. If Gabe can ride, I'll do my best. I once rode in the war for five days straight. Can't be much worse than that."

Gabe returned.

"Good to see you moving, Will. I picked some blueberries and nuts. The greatest thing for headaches and bumps on the head. Want some?"

"Sure, anything you say, Gabe. I'd even take some of that whiskey if it helped."

"Naw, best avoid that if you want to stay on a horse. This ain't the first time somebody tried to smash my head. Whiskey helps right away to dull the pain, but after, it's better to stay dry."

"All right. I'll pack up, and we'll go."

"That is woman's work. We are going to be with my people. You must get used to our ways," said Dove. "Sit and rest. Smoke with Gabe."

"When will Kajika return?"

"I do not know if he will be back. We must move whether he comes or not."

Dove saw improvement in Will and Gabe, but she was concerned about the rigors of a long ride and running into enemies.

She led Dusty over to a log and helped Will mount. Gabe shrugged her off.

"The day I can't mount my horse, I'll just sit on the front porch."

They started again, with Dove in front as before. This time both Gabe and Dove kept an eye on Will, making sure he didn't fall out of the saddle.

Dove followed the west bank of the Bighorn River, moving steadily upward. The sun was bright, the air crisp. She stayed alert but saw no signs of multiple horses passing, just the tracks of one horse, probably Kajika's mount.

They stopped to rest with the sun high in the sky; Dove again bathed the wounds of both men, though Gabe fussed at her. She thought he secretly liked the attention.

As they sat eating hardtack and jerky, Dove said, "Along this river, I remember when I was a little girl, there was a place where the water flows hot out of springs. Do you know this place?"

"Yes. I reckon it would be about two sleeps, twenty miles or so from here."

"Do you think it would be safe to camp there? Kajika said the herd is north of the band. That means they will be coming this way. If we do not hurry, perhaps we won't have to travel as far to meet them."

"Makes sense to me. I wouldn't mind soaking my bones in those springs. As long as one of us stands watch, I think it would be as safe as anywhere."

Will agreed. "I wouldn't mind a hot bath."

"The Crow regard it as sacred, so they aren't likely to bring a war party there," said Gabe.

Dove slept in her tent, not wishing to pressure Will in his weakened state, but she kept an ear out for any distress he might have in the night. For once, he seemed to sleep without dreams, and Lightning flopped by his side.

Will hung on, trying to stay with Gabe and Dove. The miles dropped behind steadily. He only had trouble once, as they ascended a steep ridge, and he had to lean forward, hanging onto the saddle horn. He saw Dove stop to wait for him, ready to dismount and help if needed. Dusty picked his way carefully, as if he knew his rider was not well.

The following day, just before the sun rose to its highest, they saw a tall bluff in the distance, across the river. They wended their way down and arrived opposite it right at noon. Steam rose from the springs, and the rock surrounding them was white. They found a grove of trees and set up camp.

Gabe agreed to take the first watch. Will gratefully went to the spring. Lightning poked a paw in the water and drew back in surprise, barking loudly. Will tested it with his hand and found it delightfully warm. He looked around and, seeing no one, stripped and climbed in, careful not to slip on the rocks. Lightning tested the water with a paw again, drew back with a yelp, and flopped on the bank.

Will laid his head back, with a silent thanks to God for this wonder of nature. He let his mind float along with his body, occasionally opening an eye to see the serene blue above or the trees moving with the gentle breeze. He lost all track of time, figuring Gabe would let him know when it was his turn. Finally, his head slipped into the water, just keeping his nose and mouth above the surface to breathe. Making sure of the footing, he even dipped below the bubbling water entirely. Will started and came up quickly when he felt something touch his leg.

Opening his eyes and pulling himself up, he saw Dove floating next to him, smiling.

"How's your head?" she asked.

"Better," he admitted. "But what are you doing here?"

"Well, there aren't exactly any other maidens to bathe with."

"You could have waited."

"Where's the fun in that? I did wait—a long time. Look at the sun!"

Will looked at the sun, then back at Dove. Her slim shoulders showed just above the water, framed by her ebony hair falling to just below her shoulder. She didn't seem to be wearing anything. It was later than he thought. He felt better, but if he got out, he'd be embarrassed. He couldn't dress quickly. He turned his back to her and pushed up on the edge until he could raise a knee to support himself and climb out. He felt self-conscious as she was probably staring at his backside, but there was no help for it. As quickly as his spinning head allowed, he got dressed and turned to see her smiling at him.

He felt the heat in his face but just said, "I'll go lie down in the shade until we're ready."

Dove smiled again, wickedly and said, "I don't know why you're worried. You're very handsome."

Will made no reply and just walked over to a fir tree.

Dove was slightly frustrated at being treated like a white woman. This morning Gabe decided she should ride in the middle for her protection with the Crow about. With Gabe's diminished eyesight and Will's weakness, Gabe was probably right. It made them feel better to think they were protecting her, but in reality, from the middle she could help either one. She slung her bow and quiver over her shoulder and mounted.

By evening, they'd just made it to the base of the red cliffs.

Gabe took the first watch. When Will wasn't looking, Dove signed to him not to call Will for the watch. She would take the duty. After setting up individual tents for her and Will, Dove gratefully took to hers, figuring he needed rest to get his strength back.

The moon was full, and the chill night air shocked her when Gabe shook her awake. She grabbed her bow, arrows, and knife and, as an afterthought, slipped Will's Navy Colt from its holster.

She went up on a point above the camp, still within easy bowshot but high enough to see the Wind River basin below. The moonlight cast many shadows, but nothing lay on the trail ahead that she could see beyond trees and rocks. She heard a coyote call, and a wolf, and wished them good hunting. Toward dawn, an owl hooted, which bothered her since that meant people had died here. As soon as the sun peeked above the horizon, she brought the fire back to a blaze and made coffee. Will had taught her a curious white man dish, flapjacks, so she made them to please him. She wanted to eat and get on the trail—she had no wish to encounter the spirits of those who had died here.

They resumed the pattern of the day before. About an hour into the journey, Gabe stopped and circled back while keeping a wary eye in front of them.

"I don't like it. I see prints of maybe a hundred horses up ahead. There's a big party of some sort up there. Prints are too muddled to tell who it is."

"Blackfeet, maybe?" said Dove.

"Maybe. Why don't you and Will stay here? I'll scout ahead, see if I can find out."

Dove quickly agreed.

Will saw a rocky outcropping just off the trail to the left, with a sheer drop of one hundred feet below it. He and Dove took cover behind the rocks. Will grabbed his Sharps and scope out of the sheath and reloaded the Navy Colt. Now they would wait.

He saw smoke rising to the southeast.

"What do you think, Dove?"

"I think there is a village, many lodges."

"What should we do if Gabe doesn't come back? If he's not back by nightfall, we should try another way, go around."

"You worry like an old woman. Gabe will be back. He was finding his way through these mountains and dealing with men wanting to take his scalp before you and I were born."

An hour passed. Then Will and Dove heard horses. Will steadied the Sharps, preparing to defend their position.

Then Dove jumped from behind cover into the open, waving excitedly. "Look! It's Gabe and some of my people. Put the rifle away!"

CHAPTER THIRTEEN

Gabe's arrival and the news of buffalo nearby put the Shoshone camp in good humor. Will couldn't quite figure out the change that came over Dove. Suddenly she was quieter, chaste, less flirty, almost like a different person. She retreated to the company of the women and rarely spoke to him unless he initiated the conversation.

Gabe took Will aside. "You need to know who's who and how to act. See that feller with the long gray-streaked hair, wearing the medallion?" he said, gesturing subtly. "That's Washakie. Don't try and shake hands. Just treat him with respect. He knows a little English, but try and use the Shoshone you have. And over there, the feller with two eagle feathers in his hair, and the big scar—that's Lone Bear, Dove's father. If you want to have her, you have to go through him. Those eagle feathers are a measure of his status. Follow me."

Gabe moved first to Washakie, greeting him in a rush of Shoshone too rapid for Will to follow. He noticed Gabe look over at him several times, gesturing. Finally, Gabe indicated he should speak.

He fumbled for the words, nervous, but in Shoshone managed, "Hello. Thank you for letting me be in your lodge."

Washakie seemed pleased and responded in English, "Welcome, friend of Gabe."

Will handed him a small pouch of tobacco, receiving a smile in return.

They walked to Lone Bear, and Gabe repeated his introduction. Will again used his limited Shoshone and gave Lone Bear the last of their sugar and a small kettle for Kimama, Dove's mother. Will felt nervous and flustered, unsure of his reception, but he wanted to make a good impression.

He noticed Kajika watched his every move. Will remembered what Dove said about jealousy—perhaps he should use caution with Kajika as well.

Washakie walked over to them and clapped Gabe on the shoulder. "Come, my friend, smoke with us," invited Washakie. "Tonight, we will celebrate finding the buffalo. Tomorrow we break camp again and move to where Kajika has seen them. Your young friend is also welcome."

Will ducked to enter the lodge and then took his place around the fire. He was surprised to see two other white men besides Gabe and himself. One, who introduced himself only as Limping Wolf, was dark-skinned, dressed in a black suit and starched collar. His spectacles, curly brown hair, and reserved manner made him seem more like Parson Breckenridge from Will's childhood in Kentucky than someone with an Indian name. The other man, perhaps ten years older than Will, red-haired, with a full beard peppered with gray, greeted Will warmly and introduced himself as James Brown, from the Salt Lake country.

The men at the fire fell into silence, which lengthened. Washakie's wife, Hanabi, brought food and passed it around. When everyone had eaten, Washakie lit a pipe, smoked, and spoke.

"My friend Gabe has come to share this last time with me. He tells me he will go to the East and never return. He has also brought back my niece Dove from her travels. I understand we owe thanks for her safety to Gabe's young friend, Will. You are welcome here, young man, so long as your heart is true and your tongue is straight. But these are troubled times; not all my Shoshone brothers will think as I do. The young men want to follow Pocatello and others who counsel war with the whites. It is a confusing time."

Brown spoke, "There is no need for war between us. We will teach you farming, and our people can become one. There will be no starving times as we help our Lamanite brothers. You won't have to move every season since the land feeds us all. Brother Brigham desires this."

"I appreciate my brother Brigham. But more of your people flood our lands. Your people kill our buffalo, capture our furs, and sometimes feed your herds upon our meadows. Your government does not protect our rights. The government does not keep its treaties and promises! We journey north now because the buffalo have not come here this year."

Limping Wolf spoke, "You do not need to abandon your ways. The Great Mystery and the Christian Father are one. You need to acknowledge His son. I can help you reason with the Great Father in Washington."

"I have lived long and always honored the ways of my fathers. The Sun provides for us; brother Buffalo feeds us. It has always been this way since the gift of horses from our Great Mystery, the chief of the sky."

Gabe spoke, "My brother Washakie speaks the truth. He is wiser than many white men."

"But the white men will not stop coming, will they?"

"No," Gabe admitted.

Turning to Will, Washakie passed him the pipe and asked, "And why are you here, my young friend? What do you seek?"

After a couple of puffs, trying not to cough, Will answered, "Peace. I have come seeking peace. I fought in the great wars of the East. I saw too many good men die instead of understanding each other. I only want a small lodge, a little ground, and a place where war cannot find me."

"Some might call that fear, but I think you have a stout heart, or Gabe would not call you friend. The whites make new roads through our lands. For myself, I do not propose to fight, even though they build this road, which will destroy many of our root grounds and drive off our game. The passage of emigrants on the new road injures us. Peace may be difficult to find."

The men smoked in silence a while longer, and then Washakie put the pipe out, signaling an end to the visit.

The dancing and celebrating went far into the night. Will slept through it after getting used to the drums, though they reminded him of artillery fire and battlefields. He prepared to move out, positioning his bedroll behind the saddle on Dusty. He'd been a little nervous that someone might take a shine to Dusty and attempt to steal him, but Gabe assured him that there was no worry. More likely, someone would try to entice Will into gambling and win him that way. Washakie himself was known to love a game of dice.

The whole village was astir. All the women busied themselves, taking down lodges, packing horses and travois, breaking camp. A few of the older men and young ones who had drunk too much the night before were idle, but everyone else was moving.

Dove approached Will almost shyly and left him a package of dried meat for the journey. She didn't even speak—just waved when he tried to talk to her.

Young men were sent out to scout the herd's present location, Kajika among them. Within an hour, they reported back that the buffalo were not far now, only a little north of Ocean Lake.

Will was amazed at the efficiency with which the whole camp moved. He'd seen military units that moved slower. Within an hour, the entire band was traveling in the direction of the buffalo herd.

The days of rest had done good things for him. He felt well, just an occasional twinge in the head that reminded him of his collision with rocks in the river. Will decided that as soon as they made camp, he'd find a place to test his marksmanship and see how he was progressing.

He could only understand snatches of the jocular conversation among the men as they rode. Each one seemed to be joking, boasting, or teasing one of the others about their prospects for the hunt. Most of the men carried old rifled muskets and carbines. All had bow and arrows.

When they arrived at the chosen campsite by a stream, everything went in reverse, with the women setting up the lodges and the men making a sweat lodge where they could fast and pray to the sun for the success of the hunt. The sweat lodge consisted of a dome-shaped frame of saplings covered by heavy buffalo robes, with a small hole at the top in the center to act as a chimney, releasing steam and smoke. A fire would burn in the center, heating rocks, with water dumped on them every few minutes, causing steam.

Will rode Dusty a distance from the camp, away from everyone, to a natural draw surrounded on three sides with bluffs along the stream. He made sure the Colt was loaded and took out the Sharps with the Malcolm scope. He inspected and cleaned the Sharps, re-assembled it, and paced off twenty yards, one hundred yards, then three hundred yards, setting up targets at the locations.

The targets were just rocks set on top of one another, for lack of anything better. Will went back to the firing line and started with the Colt, taking careful aim at the closest target. He checked his breathing and fired. Dirt puffed just below the target. He adjusted and fired again, this time hitting the target, and then shot three times more in rapid succession, kicking the rock farther along. He relaxed, holstered the Colt, and picked up the Sharps, bracing it on a tree stump.

He aimed at the hundred-yard target and fired. He hit a little low and left, adjusted, and fired three more rounds, each blasting the rock target. He quickly re-focused to the farthest mark. He reloaded and fired, striking dead center each time.

He was ready. He spent the rest of the morning in prayer and reading his Bible.

Just as the sun reached its highest point, the warriors mounted to go on the hunt. Washakie and Gabe were not going, content to let the younger men have the glory.

Will prepared to join the hunt but was brought up short by Kajika.

"You will bring bad luck. You haven't been to the sweat lodge. You're white. You don't know anything. You don't need the meat, but our people will starve without it. Besides," he said, gesturing contemptuously at the Sharps, "there is nothing brave about hunting with such a gun. You are like the whites in the East that shoot buffalo from iron wagons. Anyone could do it. My little sister could kill a buffalo with such a gun."

Will noticed Kajika carried a bow, arrows, and lance.

Washakie and Gabe happened by, laughing together. Washakie stopped, took in the situation, and gave Kajika a cold stare.

Kajika stared back defiantly for a moment, then broke and muttered, "Come, then. A bull may gore your horse."

Will noticed Dove standing under a tree. When he looked at her, she held his gaze a moment, but he could not read her eyes. She turned away, moving back toward the other women. Neither Limping Wolf nor Brown made any attempt to join the hunt.

The warriors formed a semicircle around the herd. The cows on the fringe looked up, protective of their calves, but then resumed eating. The men avoided quick movements until everyone was in position. Will remembered Gabe's parting words.

"You don't have to do this, son. Washakie will treat you as a guest, no matter what, on my account. But if you're determined, then do it to gain honor, Shoshone style. Use your rifle only at great need. You'll see men using muskets, but we both know that ain't the same. Use your Colt. You'll have to get close. They will think you're something if you can touch a cow, not fall off and get trampled, and make a few kills. It ain't so much how many as how you go about it. Just remember, if you fall off, you're dead."

Will fell in line, by habit, at the back of the group of warriors. He rode Dusty carefully to within about thirty feet of two grazing cows. He looked out at the herd. The plain was black with them, probably a thousand adult bison plus their calves from last year.

The waiting was tense. Controlled excitement filled the air, like a cannon waiting to explode.

Suddenly the hunt leader gave a loud "Yip Yip Yip." All the braves went into action at once, whooping, shooting, charging the herd. The herd began to move, cows bellowing and calves crying. The earth thundered with the movement. Will surged forward. Dusty wanted to run, caught up in the excitement, but Will held him to a controlled lope. A young bull whirled and seemed about to charge from the side. Will fired three times, striking the head, the heart, and a leg. The bull went down.

He turned his attention forward just in time to see a cow lunge at him. He pulled Dusty sharply to the right, pivoting hard and avoiding the horns. Now Will had cows on both sides, a more dangerous position. Up ahead, he saw Kajika put a lance into a cow, who went down. Will moved right, a risk if a cow suddenly swerved toward him. She seemed to run with him in a straight line. He leaned right in the saddle until the revolver was only two feet from her head and fired. The cow moved forward on inertia and then went down. Will swerved farther right, away from the herd. With no one behind him, he pulled up to give Dusty a breather.

Looking out over the herd, he saw Kajika with his bow in hand, the arrow on the string, aiming at a large cow with an almost black hump. Just in front of that cow was another young warrior, concentrating his aim on a buffalo farther in front. Kajika released the arrow, and the big cow surged forward, horns grazing the mount of the young warrior. The horse shied and stumbled. Will acted on instinct. In one fluid motion, he brought the Sharps up to eye level, aimed, and fired. The big cow went down, creating a small island that the other animals surged around. The young warrior crouched behind his fallen horse, using it for a shield. Kajika moved forward and offered the man a lift up behind him. Once mounted, they loped out of the herd and circled back toward camp. Will decided to follow.

Surely two kills were enough for one day.

Back in camp, Will went to Kajika.

"Is he all right?" Will asked of the young warrior.

"Yes, my brother Lame Deer is all right—no thanks to you! You shot that cow. I could have saved him. You took my kill and my honor."

Will was shocked. "Hey, no need to be upset. I was trying to help."

"I told you that you were bad luck. Go away; you've done enough."

Will retreated to Washakie's lodge and found Dove waiting for him at the entrance.

"I heard that you killed two. Washakie is pleased. Since you have no wife to do the skinning and drying, as is proper, Washakie suggested I do it for you. That is if you don't mind."

"Mind? Of course not. It's an honor. Can I . . . see you later? After the party tonight? I want to talk."

"All right. Down by the creek, near where the horses water. Can you hoot like an owl? That would keep everyone away."

"I can try. Thank you!"

Dove took her skinning knife, an ax, and a crude saw with her. After Will showed her where his kills were and returned to camp, she built a frame to dry the skins. Then began the arduous task of butchering the two buffalo. Will made it clear that the cow was for Kajika.

Butchering and preparing the hides gave her time to think. The process of butchering took strength, but not much thought. She'd been doing it since girlhood. Here, she had little freedom and constant work. She'd always been her parents' difficult child, full of mischief, wanting to do things the boys did, and trying new things. Once, a few of the other mothers banded together to talk to her mother about her behavior. Now, Will had to be wondering about the change in the way she acted. She knew she had to conform, but she didn't know how long she could manage.

Will had said he wanted to talk. She could only imagine what was on his mind—probably marriage. But here, she had to consider her family. What about her father? What about Kajika? She wanted Will. If only her father would approve. He'd done well in the hunt, showing he could provide. But still, he was white. If she ran away again with Will, her father might come after them.

She liked living in her band—except for the restrictive life of women. She smiled, remembering her joyous reunion with her sister, Laughing Moon, who, at fourteen summers, would be marrying soon. Their girlhood joys would not last much longer when Laughing Moon had her own lodge.

She paused to saw off a haunch, pick up the hide, and stretch it on the frame she had built. Will might not be quite as handsome as Kajika. But he was kind and brave. She would never lack for meat with him around. When he kissed her, really kissed her, her knees went weak. He had the whites' odd ideas about making love, but that could change. She could honor his God. Wasn't it just that the Great Mystery and his son were one?

But would Will stay here? Or would he want to go back among the whites? What if the whites came and surrounded them? Or worse, what if they came to fight? Would Will fight against the whites to defend her and their children?

Kajika was . . . well, predictable. All Shoshone warrior. He expected a woman to be his bed mate and do his bidding. His muscles stood out on his chest and arms. She knew he would want to dominate, to control, even possess her. There would be lots of children. Her rebellious streak might provoke beatings. What if he tired of her? Most Shoshone only took one wife, but some took more. If the union didn't work out, separation was possible, but who would want a woman cast off by another man? Most women just endured their unhappy lot.

The thought of sharing her lodge with another wife made her angry. She scraped the hide so hard she almost made a hole.

Dove made up her mind—she must teach Will their customs so that her father would favor him. If he didn't insist on returning to white society, where she would never be accepted, they could be happy together.

Evening around the fires brought celebration, dancing, and boasting among the men of their prowess in the hunt. Dove stood back with the other women, attending to calls for food and drink. She felt exhausted after the work of butchering the two carcasses. She had done as Will requested, offering the tongue and liver of each beast—the best parts—to Washakie and Kajika. Kajika had spurned the offer, and she had given them to her father instead.

"Father, I need to go and collect more wood. I'll be back soon."

Her father nodded and waved her off, listening to Kajika's brother tell about how the herd almost ran over him

Dove slipped away in the direction of the horse herd, looking for Will. She figured no one would notice either of them amid the celebration, except possibly Gabe. She found Will scanning the stars, sitting cross-legged about half a bow-shot from the herd.

"Will? You wanted to talk. I'm sorry if I've seemed distant since we've been home, but I must respect my father and the customs of my people. I can't seem too familiar with you in public."

"I assumed as much. But now that we're here, I have decisions to make, decisions that concern you. I promised to see you home safe, and I've done that, though I wondered a few times whether I was keeping you safe or vice versa. We did it together. I heard Gabe say he will be leaving soon for the East and doesn't expect to return. You know I love you.

"But we have some things to work out . . . First, where do I stand with you? Second, if we . . . if I . . . well, we need to understand one another about beliefs. I don't want a relationship with you that doesn't last. We do have a preacher here, it seems, for a real wedding."

"I love you, Will. I don't know how my father will see our relationship. I don't know if he will approve. The Salt Lake people much influence him and Washakie, but they also respect our old ways. I want to be with you to be your wife. I know you are a good and true man, but they do not."

Will's eyes barely cracked open the next morning after the celebration. Shaking himself, he rose and dressed.

Will walked over to Gabe, who was packing.

"Gabe, I want to thank you . . . for everything! You taught me so much."

"You're a good man. I reckon you can survive on your own now. I have to get back to St. Louis while I can still see to do it. Durndest thing, my eyes are going bad on me. Washakie will watch out for you as long as you stay straight and on his good side. Just be aware—he ain't no pussycat. He once saved his people from a war by doing individual combat, with the winner to eat the other's heart. He won, and he done it. Keep your hair! And that gal . . . don't forget she's his niece," Gabe said as he mounted. He led a packhorse, given to him by Washakie, with plenty of buffalo meat and hides.

Will waved as the old mountain man left the camp, attended by shouting children and Washakie walking with him to the edge of the village.

Will turned and moved back to the fire at the center of the camp, where broad hindquarters of buffalo were slowly smoking on a spit. He held out his hands to warm them. James Brown, the

Mormon missionary, joined him at the fire.

"You're new to the Shoshone, the Snake?" said James.

"I guess you could say so. I've been around Dove for almost a year, learned some from her and Old Gabe. This is my first time in a Shoshone village."

"And are you planning to stay?"

"My plans are my own and a bit indefinite."

"Ah, I see. Well, I just thought I should tell you that Brother Brigham has directed us to share the faith with our Shoshone brothers and bring them into the fold by marrying their daughters. They may be the Laminites, from when our Lord visited these shores, but we can sanctify them through marriage. I've made a proposal to Lone Bear concerning your friend Dove, and he is considering it. I'm sure my wife would welcome her."

Will felt as if Brown had punched him in the gut. "Your wife? You're already married?"

"Of course, many souls are waiting for bodies. It is permitted to have many wives so that there will be many children. The children will become sanctified, whiter, and eventually gods of their worlds. I've offered Lone Bear a string of good ponies, many sacks of grain, and a farm with our people."

"Does Dove know anything about this?"

"She doesn't need to know. She will follow the will of her father, as befits a woman."

"You don't know her very well, do you?"

"And you don't know the Shoshone. Just a friendly warning," said James, moving off.

Will's first reaction was shock, then anger, then determination. He thought all he'd have to worry about was Lone Bear and possibly Kajika. This threat was unexpected.

That night, the weather was good, and he slept outdoors on his bedroll, near Dusty, as he used to do in the war. The Wyoming night sky with millions of stars stretched out before him. It brought to mind the Bible verses, "When I consider thy heavens, the work of thy fingers, the moon, and the stars, which thou hast ordained; What is man, that thou art mindful of him? And the son of man, that thou visitest him?"

Where was God in what he was doing? If he was supposed to marry Dove, why weren't things coming together? But he couldn't just roll over—what if James bribed her father? Somehow Will had to get Lone Bear's attention. But how? All he had was his guns, horse, a few camping supplies, and a few silver coins. Could he do some act of courage that would raise his status with Lone Bear? He didn't want more killing, but maybe something more that showed him a worthy provider. Then there was the niggling voice at the back of his mind that made him wonder—would staying here with Dove be the peace he sought? And if not, what then?

He prayed and mulled it over until sleep came.

After the morning meal, Kajika came to Will. Will looked up curiously, wondering what he could want—he'd avoided him most of the time Will had been there.

"White man, some here think you are a great warrior. It wouldn't be fair to fight you—your hair would grace my lodge, and there is no honor in defeating a woman. My people often love a good contest, especially with a wager. I have many fine horses, but I like yours. He might even be fit for one of the Lakota to steal. At least he could pull a travois with my lodge. If you race me on my best horse, the winner can take the losing horse. If you are the warrior Gabe claims, it should be no trouble for you. You can always steal another from the Crow.”

Will wondered if this was a trap. If he refused, he would have no honor. His eyes narrowed. “How do I know your horse is worth it? Or that you’d keep your word?”

Kajika laughed. “How do you know I won’t kill you and take everything anyway? Your protector is gone,” he said, motioning in the direction Gabe had taken.

Will felt anger rise, but he suppressed it, knowing that to become angry was to give his opponent an advantage.

“Gabe was a friend, never a protector. My protector is my God.”

Will thought and prayed a moment, and, sensing that to refuse would cause him to lose honor, he said, “All right. I’ll race you. But if I win, I get to choose the two best of your horses.”

Kajika spat. “All right, little man. I will take your horse after the race. Perhaps when Washakie has tired of you, I’ll hang your scalp on my lodge.”

“We’ll see. I’ve often heard it is better to have less thunder in the mouth and more lightning in the hand.”

Will watched as Kajika went and delivered a similar challenge to James Brown. He heard part of it as he followed Kajika over to where Brown was making coffee outside his tent.

“Think of it as a contest between the Great Mystery and your Mormon god. Brother Wolf will give me the speed of a sunbeam. Of course, if you’re afraid you’ll lose . . .”

“I’ll be there!” snapped Brown.

Dove was down at the river, fetching water in a pottery jar. As she straightened, she saw someone coming from the village. She hoped it was Will, but she was careful not to make any sound that might give him away. As she walked closer with the jar on her shoulder, she saw it was the man from the Lake of Salt, Brown. She took two steps out of the path to avoid him, but he followed.

"I've been looking for you, Dove."

"Me? Why?"

"I've asked your father for your hand. I have much to give. I'm hoping that you'll come with me to talk to him."

"Why would I do that? I hardly know you."

"I'm not a hard man. You'll know that in time. Come."

"And if I refuse?"

"I've offered your father land, horses, grain. You can't possibly turn me down for that no-account rebel. And sealed to me, there will be much profit for both our peoples. Kajika and Crump want to race me for a horse. But they cannot win. I've heard that you turned down Kajika once already, and your father let it stand. You will be mine whether you come now or later." He grabbed her, pulling her close enough for his hot breath to fill her nostrils, and she could see a red splotch on his face.

Dove wrenched loose and dumped the jug of water on Brown. It shattered, and she ran around him, back to the village.

As the sun rose higher the next morning, Will, Kajika, and Brown all came to the starting line for the race. They made Lone Bear and Washakie the judges, and already betting in the village reached a fever pitch.

Dove heard conjectures that if Will lost, he would try again and bet his rifle. Everyone knew that Lone Bear was making up his mind. Her heart hammered her ribs. She looked at the other horses. Kajika had almost been born on horseback, learning to ride soon after he could walk. His horse had the spotted rear of the Nez Perce tribe, with big, powerful hindquarters and the ability to turn quickly. Gabe had told stories about them. Brown's was a long-limbed chestnut that looked built for distance. Dove had warned Will about the chestnut, and the course was set at about four bow-shots out and then back. None of the riders was using a saddle. Will had the advantage of weighing less than the other two, but Kajika was more used to riding bareback.

She couldn't stand the thought of Brown winning. Without a horse, what would Will do? And he would lose stature with her father. She might be subject to a white man as the second wife. Dove couldn't understand how her father could even think of allowing Brown to take her. Hadn't the Salt Lake people refused to give their daughters to the Shoshone? If Brown won, perhaps she and Will would have to risk running away. Maybe there was somewhere that no one would care if she wasn't white. Oh, Will just had to win!

Everyone in the village turned out in a line at the edge of the course. Lots of good-natured jesting was going on. Kajika was the favorite. The young men whooped their approval when he mounted. There was a tree at the other end of the course. Will guessed it might be a quarter of a mile to the tree. The horses would go around it and return. The first back was the winner.

Before Will mounted, Limping Wolf came over to him.

"My son, you have made this a contest before God. I have prayed for you. But know that these men will stop at nothing. I wonder, though, is it wise for you to do this? You might end up on foot, in a land with no friends. She that you seek is not a believer. She may not leave the ways of her people, even if you convince Lone Bear. There may be a terrible choice."

"Thanks, padre. I'm counting on you to marry us. Didn't the

disciples seek guidance by casting lots? I guess that's what I'm doing. I have to go."

"Go with God."

Will jumped up on Dusty. What Limping Wolf said bothered him, but he pushed it out of his mind. He looked over at Dove, surrounded by her mother and siblings. He saw hope and pleading in her gaze. He tried to look confident and calm, but he was sweating in the chill morning air. Why couldn't Kajika have picked a shooting contest?

Dusty pranced nervously, picking up on Will's tension. The others were mounted. He watched the brave designated to fire the starting shot and braced for Dusty's acceleration. At this distance, the turn was the only place Dusty would slow.

The shot set Will's blood racing as he dug his heels into Dusty and gave him his head. Dusty responded with instant speed, hitting full stride in a second. Will concentrated on the tree mark but noticed Kajika was ahead of him. The ground was rough, and Kajika would know every inch of it. Rocks and bushes flew by. Will looked at the ground in front, mostly trusting Dusty to pick his way but watching for anything that might throw him off stride. Kajika was a full length ahead now, and Will could hear Brown's horse on his left, head almost up to Dusty's hindquarters. The cheering and jeering behind them faded as they neared the tree. Just as they were about to turn, Kajika swerved his horse directly in front of Will and pulled back on him, then shifted quickly into the turn. Will had to pull up on Dusty to avoid a collision. The lost momentum cost him. As they started the return trip, Brown's horse came up to Dusty's neck. Now Kajika was almost two lengths ahead. Abandoning all caution, Will urged Dusty to give everything. Kajika's Appaloosa was beginning to tire, but Kajika used the rawhide bridle as a whip.

The distance was favoring Brown's horse now. He drew even with Dusty. Then it happened—Dusty stumbled a step, and Brown's horse pulled ahead. Will struggled to retain his balance, leaning forward over Dusty's neck. He thought of Dove and prayed, "God help me!"

Dusty regained his stride, and Will pushed him, whooping a rebel yell and pounding his sides with his heels. He leaned forward, his seat urging Dusty. They began to gain, first up to Brown's legs, then even, then passing him. Dusty shot ahead. The finish was close now, maybe a hundred yards.

Dusty seemed to understand and gained more. Will had never flown this fast, even with Federal troops chasing him. They reached the Appaloosa's hindquarters. Thirty yards to go. Dusty continued to gain. Kajika swung the rawhide at Dusty's head, causing a swerve. Will held tight to a hunk of mane and used the extra distance from the swerve to keep away from Kajika, kicking Dusty again. Suddenly they were even, and Will could see the crowd and the finish just ahead. It seemed like Dusty pulled ahead as the finish passed by, but Will couldn't tell.

He slowed Dusty and walked him. Maybe it would be his last time riding Dusty. Would Lone Bear and Washakie be fair? Had he even really won? He was shaking, and Dusty dripped with lather when he slid off. He looked and saw Dove running toward him, smiling and crying at the same time.

"Father says you won. Only by a nose. Washakie agrees. You won!" She threw her arms around him and kissed him in front of everyone.

CHAPTER FOURTEEN

Again that night, there was much dancing and feasting. Will went and claimed his prizes, two good horses from each of his rivals, along with a pound of tobacco and sugar from James Brown for coming in last. Will sat between Lone Bear and Dove's brother at the feast, a seat of honor. Once Kajika had given him the horses, Kajika mounted and rode away. On Dove's advice, Will did not claim the Appaloosa, Kajika's best horse, as was his right. He took a mare and a stallion and another two mares from Brown. He was exhausted from the tension and the physical exertion of the race. At the fire, the men expected him to smoke, to sample the native drink, and to tell the story of the race. Two of the men made him offers for Dusty, but he turned them down.

He wanted to ask Lone Bear about Dove, but she'd cautioned him not to be too hasty or push too soon. He did as everyone wished and then went to his bedroll after a brief hug from Dove. He guessed it might be midnight.

In the morning, he found that Brown had left, pleading illness, and had gone back to Salt Lake. He played a game a little like stickball with Dove's brother and some of the other young boys. At noon, Laughing Moon called them to eat, including Will. He felt elated but restrained his enthusiasm.

He sat quietly in the family circle and accepted the pipe after offering a few ounces of the tobacco to his host. He could smoke without coughing now, but he still hated the taste, the burning in his throat.

Lone Bear spoke, "Where did you get such a horse? I've never seen one like him."

Dove translated.

"My sister and her husband bought him for me from a farm in Kentucky, my family's home beyond the great river. After the great war, I returned home, but my family's lodge burned, and there was nothing left. I went to find my parents, but it was not the same."

"Men came and burned your home and drove you out of your land?"

"Burned the farm, yes. They didn't drive me out, but my family moved on, and there wasn't any way to start over. Farming never really appealed to me. I had a lot of bad memories of the war. Death, friends lost, men killed. Many battles. I came to find peace, maybe a place where I can be with the mountains, the sky, the animals. Then I found your daughter."

He passed the pipe back to Lone Bear, who sat silently, smoking and reflecting.

"We have had whites here before. Washakie had a white boy who lived as his son for a time. But then he returned to his people and came no more. I do not want my daughter to be poor or hungry. The whites at the Salt Lake want her to come, but I think Kajika speaks the truth when he says the whites just want to use their guns and religion to control us. I saw the whites slaughter my village. I am old. I will not see many more winters. The lake whites wish to take her spirit away from her people. Will I see my grandchildren? Will they treat her well? Or will she be a slave to them? And you, you may take her somewhere I will never see her again. If she dies, you will put her in the ground, so her spirit is not free to join her ancestors."

"Lone Bear, I don't want to go far away. I want to live here in peace, in the mountains. If other white men come, I can help. I can make their talk, help them to understand how the Shoshone think. I can hunt. I even know how to farm, if it comes to that."

"I will think on these things. If you stay here, you must become a warrior—someone in tune with the Great Mystery. Your medicine must be strong enough to overcome hers, or there will be no children. You need to go on a hunt. You must bring me the hide of a mountain sheep, the hide of a cougar, and three bald eagle feathers. You will only use a knife and a pistol. Kajika will do the same hunt with Shoshone weapons. If the Great Mystery brings you success, more than Kajika, I will consider the match. Then I will know you can provide for my daughter. If the Great Mystery smiles on Kajika, then he will be her husband. If you stay, you would need a new name. You need to do the sweat lodge for purification. You should think about these things."

Will sat in the sweat lodge, thinking and praying. With no one there to notice, he pounded the bench he sat on in frustration. He'd gained the horses needed to make a gift to Lone Bear to increase his standing in the tribe, and at considerable risk. He'd made an enemy of Kajika, but Will still didn't have permission to marry Dove. He'd agreed to go on the hunt despite a nagging voice in the back of his head that told him that even then, it might not be enough. Why did everything have to be so complicated? Yet he'd observed how Dove was since she got home to her people—she was happy. And wasn't that what they'd worked so hard to accomplish, to get her home safe? It was clear that his original idea of just making a little cabin somewhere on a mountain lake and living undisturbed had been naive. He'd had no idea about tribal warfare and the hate that many tribes now had for white men. Wasn't he just another one? Whites came claiming land, killing game, and challenging their ways. If he tried to achieve his vision, they'd probably only last until the next Sioux or Blackfoot war party found them. Maybe peace wasn't a place.

It seemed like his options were to join the Shoshone, go back to his family, or risk making it on his own, without knowing whether he'd be as capable or fortunate as Gabe, and wasn't the man already a legend? Or he could join the crowd of settlers in Oregon.

He emerged from the sweat lodge as the sun angled downward in the west. He prepared for the hunt. Searching through saddlebags, he couldn't find his flint and steel for fires. Instead, he came across the magnifying glass he'd bought, intending to give it to Old Gabe to help his eyes. He remembered something he'd learned at Transylvania College—lenses could make fire!

He needed to dry some strips of venison to eat after his fast ended. He cleared some ground near the horses and took the magnifying glass, pointing the sun's rays at some dry grass and pine needles.

Dove and a few others came over to see what he was doing. There was some good-natured ribbing about the crazy white man. After a few minutes, some drifted off, but others, having nothing better to do, stayed to watch.

The grass started smoking and burst into flame.

"Look! He makes fire with Father Sun!"

They looked at him in awe and fear—even Dove backed up. Will didn't understand all the commotion.

"What's wrong, Dove?"

She looked at him, mouth wide open in surprise. "You have the power of the sun! I did not know. This is big medicine!"

Will knew better than to laugh. "It's nothing—just some glass in the right shape, a sunny day, and a little time. I couldn't find my flint and steel. I was too embarrassed to ask for your fire drill." He held up the magnifying glass.

"I meant to give this to Gabe to help him read better. With all the excitement from the hunt, I forgot about it."

"I must tell my father of this—he will want to know! When will you leave for your hunt?"

"As soon as I can. I'll take my bedroll if that's allowed, and my pistol. Can we talk for a while?"

Dove paused, coughing hard and bringing her hands to her throat.

Will asked, "Are you all right?"

She switched to English. "Yes, but we must not talk alone. There would be gossip. If we speak English, few here will understand."

"All right, if you're sure you are well. Dove, you know I want to marry you. I'm willing to stay here. But we need to think alike on matters of the spirit. Your father wants me to learn the Shoshone way, and I'm willing—to a point. But I also want you to understand my people, my ways. Our people agree on the beginning of the world and the great flood. My people think all the bad in the world came from not following the Great Mystery's commandments. That's why the great flood came. But then God sent his Son, born as a human baby, to earth and named him Jesus. When someone does wrong, God punishes the wrong; after they die, they go to a horrible place forever. But God loves everyone and doesn't want people to have to go to the place of fire, so he sent his Son, Jesus, to die for us. Jesus was different, like in your stories, he was one with God, so he never did anything wrong.

"My people believe that you have to admit that you make mistakes, you do wrong things, but you're willing to accept that Jesus came to take the punishment for those mistakes, that he died, but the Great Mystery brought him back to life. If you are willing to believe this, then God will live with you, and you never have to go to the bad place. God also says not to marry someone who doesn't believe this."

Dove shook her head slowly. "I don't understand all that. I've heard some things like it from the black robes and different things from the lake people. All I know is I love you. You say you love me— isn't that enough?"

"I wish it were. But I cannot be someone I am not. What do you love about me?"

She lowered her eyes, then said, "I love your body, the way it feels to kiss and hold you. I love that you fight and are not afraid. I love that you help. You care about those that are weaker. I love your honesty and even your stubbornness, though it drives me crazy sometimes."

"Don't you see, those things that you love about me come from my faith, my relationship with the Great Mystery, and His son, Jesus?"

"Yes . . . I know you try to do the right thing always, even when it is hard."

"It's more than that. Jesus forgives us all the wrong things that we do if we ask him. He wants us to forgive and love too—even the things my people have done to your people."

"Washakie says that holding hate in your heart rots it."

"Can you believe that Jesus came to take all the evil of men onto himself? That all may be forgiven? We all deserve punishment for the hate and wrong things in our lives. I know that when I turn from bad things and confess to them, he can make my life new. He can for you too."

"I want this Jesus of yours."

Will prayed with her, asking Jesus to take away the hurt and hate.

Dove closed her eyes, following his example, and prayed after him, "Jesus, come and live with me."

Looking up again, she said, "I feel . . . peaceful. Like the Great Mystery has visited me. I will ask him to help you be successful and to protect you. Be careful. Kajika is still angry. He does not know Jesus. He may try to harm you."

Will gathered his things, finding Lightning waiting outside the lodge. It was now late afternoon.

Will had his Bible, his rifle, a bedroll, a box of cartridges, Dove's knife, his magnifying glass, a waterskin, a rope, and a small amount of jerked venison to break his fast. He'd had nothing to eat since morning.

Lone Bear and Dove came to see him off. Will noticed that Dove seemed not herself. There were beads of sweat on her forehead, though the day was chilly. She had a red spot on her face that hadn't been there earlier in the day.

Kajika stood off to the side, carrying a bow and a war club.

Lone Bear said, "Do you see the cliffs? That is Wolverine Peak. Go that direction, and then wherever the Great Mystery leads you. The mountain sheep often go there. No horse could climb it. Your mind and spirit will cleanse in hardship."

"I'll be waiting for you," Dove said, smiling.

Will left the village going southwest. Lightning trotted steadily beside him. It pained him to leave Dusty, but Lone Bear assured him he would keep the horse safe. Kajika went a different way. He must gain his prizes and return before Kajika. Rocks, logs, pine seedlings, lichen, and small animals were everywhere. The sky was beginning to cloud over, and the terrain sloped upward, gently at first, then more sharply. He kept what Lone Bear had called Wolverine Peak in view. He would camp before reaching the top and light a fire while the sun was still above the horizon.

On the outcropping ahead, he saw a bighorn sheep, still like stone, staring at him. His first prize! Moving slowly, he inched his way toward the animal. A falcon circled high overhead, gazing down, seeking dinner. The sheep turned and scrambled up some rocks layered in strata, with barely a foothold, like a man climbing a ladder.

Will's stomach began to growl. Plodding on, he ascended another two hundred feet, and he found a flat place with a little protection from the wind. The sheep looked down at him and bleated as if to laugh at his puny progress. Should he just camp for the night, try tomorrow? Soon he wouldn't have the sun to build a fire. The clouds mingled pink and orange. Just ahead, there was a widening of the path with a rock wall on one side and a large boulder on the other. The sheep was about twenty-five yards ahead, up two levels of rock. Just beyond were sheltering boulders—he wouldn't get two shots. Will knelt and braced the revolver on a boulder, sighting upward as the sun sank behind the peak. The sheep bleated again and jumped for the next level up, just as Will fired. The sound reverberated through the canyon. The acrid smell of gunpowder blew away on the wind as the shot hit in the hindquarter, causing the sheep to lose his footing, falling to the path. Will raced over after holstering his gun and ended it with the knife Dove had given him. He'd obtained the sheep, but what of bears, which might smell the kill?

Will gathered tinder and kindling, moving out into the sun to catch the fading rays. He remembered what Dove had said about Kajika. The fire was a risk, but without fire and no tent to protect from the Wyoming wind, he'd freeze. He coaxed the smoking grass, and a gust came that blew it out.

A coyote howled somewhere nearby, and Will thought of Dove's Coyote stories, how he was always a trickster, causing men trouble. He must be letting this superstition stuff get to his head. Remembering his war experience, he knew not to rush the fire, even though the sun was sinking lower quickly. Finally, he got sparks, some smoke, and then a small blaze, which he tended carefully. He piled up kindling, then larger branches, then a few fallen logs that were near the edge of the path. Dove had talked of hardship—it looked like he was going to have his share.

He dragged the sheep over near the fire and began skinning. It was full dark by the time he finished, bagged up the horns and skin, and roasted some of the meat. Regretfully he decided to push most of the carcass over the cliff for the scavengers. He couldn't risk keeping it, and he couldn't carry it on the rest of the hunt. He wondered if Kajika had also found one of the animals.

It was too dark to read his Bible. Using a rock for a pillow, he lay on his back, looking at the stars. A shooting star lit the sky in a streak. He remembered Dove saying that the points of light in the night sky were people in many cases, who'd been placed there by Coyote. Others were thought to be large campfires, lit for the spirits of the departed to keep them warm in the after world. She had pointed out a group of five, who were supposedly warriors. The five formed the shape of a canoe in the sky. The story said that the warriors were building a canoe and planned to send it out on the big lake. Blue Jay heard their plans but, flying far and high, saw a storm coming that would surely drown them if they were out on the lake. Blue Jay flew to Coyote with her concerns about her friends, but Coyote said he could not help them on the lake. The best he could do would be to put them in the Sky World. Coyote lifted the men and the canoe into the sky, and they still work together there every night.

He also remembered the Bible said that Jesus had given each star a name. He and God had created them.

Will's thinking turned to drowsiness, and he slept. Lightning curled up next to him. He woke up twice, hungry and a little cold, stoked up the fire again, leaned into Lightning for warmth, and tried for more sleep. He heard a chuffing noise, like a bear. Lightning jumped up, alert, sniffing the air, but then lay down as it moved away.

In a dream, a wolf came near the fire but did not growl or attack. Instead, like Dove's stories, the wolf could talk. The wolf asked him, "What are you doing here, little one? You are not one of my people."

When dawn came, he stretched stiff legs, rolled to a kneeling position, and wished for coffee. Since there was none, he took a sip from the waterskin, and the icy coldness of it helped shock him awake. There wasn't much to pack beyond the sheepskin and horns, so he was on his way, moving toward the summit of Wolverine Peak within a few minutes. The path grew steeper, and he slipped on small pebbles.

After two hours of climbing, the skies grew dark and lightning flashed. A gentle rain spattered on the brim of Will's hat then fell harder. After about ten minutes, it roared down in a torrent, with thunder and wind that made the drops feel like needles. There was a lake ahead with a rocky outcropping near the shore. Will flattened himself against a rock under the outcropping, not moving. A large rock tottered above and fell to the path, crashing just in front of him. Lightning heard the rumble and jumped aside. Will was getting soaked and cold. After what seemed like forever, the storm blew itself out. Lightning whimpered, pushing in next to him.

The wind dropped to a breeze, and he moved out to assess the damage. His clothes and bedroll were soaked. The oilskin around his cartridges had kept them dry, but he would need to clean the revolver to prevent rust. He slicked back his hair with one hand and twisted the water out of his hat, then worked it back into shape on his head.

He trudged onward, the temperature dropping as the elevation rose. He wondered if the bits of grass he'd saved from the night before would still be dry inside the pouch with the dried sheep meat. He was hungry enough to chew rocks—he'd gotten used to plenty to eat. He tore off a small piece of the meat, and Lightning devoured it.

His feet made squishing sounds in his boots as he toiled upward. After another two hours, he was at a steep, narrow wash. It went up sharply, with a treacherous footing of loose rock and ice. Up in the air ahead, he saw an eagle circle and then land on the side of a cliff. It must be where the nest was. He struggled up about fifty feet and slipped, falling and sliding downward. Lightning barked and pranced—he couldn't follow Will. His hand smashed the rock and drew blood. When he regained his footing, he struggled on to a ledge where he could stop and bandage the hand. Fortunately, it was his left, not his shooting hand.

Looking down, he called to Lightning, "Stay there, boy. I don't know if you can understand it. I'll be back as soon as I can."

Lightning barked and danced about, finally laying down.

He rested and surveyed the terrain, looking for a route to the top. Grabbing finger holds, he pulled his way up, boots tentatively searching for solid crevices. With his injured left hand, he took out Dove's knife, driving it into the cliff face of soil and ice, using it for leverage, even though it throbbed. Crawling on hands and knees, he moved steadily up, using the knife to help pull himself up the slope. The cold made the blood on his hands congeal. He felt rather than saw his trouser leg rip at the bottom on sharp rocks. Foot by foot, he went up until he pulled himself onto a plateau that ran along the top. There was no cover, and the wind hammered him. Using rocks as weights, he stretched out the bedroll to dry, letting the wind blast over it. Unless the gale let up, he didn't know how he would have a fire. But if the wind ceased, how would he get dry? Would he freeze in his damp clothing? Would Lightning wait for him?

It was too close to dark to try roping down the cliff to the eagle's nest. He'd have to wait for morning.

There was no wood, but there were rocks. The wind came from the northwest. He set to work piling stones into a three-sided shelter with walls nearly a foot thick, facing east, away from the wind. He couldn't make a roof, but at least there could be a windbreak.

As the sun dipped behind the peaks, he ventured out of his makeshift shelter and tested the bedroll. It was dry enough, drier than his clothes. He brought it inside the walls and quickly took off all his clothing, weighing it with rocks to keep it from blowing away, and then wrapped himself in the bedroll.

After a time, the moon came out. The wind faded and became a whisper. He rose, teeth chattering and checked his clothing, which was still there. He dressed, again wrapped in the bedroll, and waited. Hunger gnawed through to his backbone. He was weary, even having slept a little, and had sore bones and muscles that he hadn't known existed. He didn't know what he expected to happen. What if the eagle wasn't there and didn't come back?

The dawn came, and a gentle chinook blew, warming the ridge. The clouds vanished, leaving bright blue as far as he could see. The eagle lazily circled, heading for a nearby lake far below. Ground squirrels and mice skittered about, seeking their morning food. Had his climb been for nothing?

Will thought suddenly of the verse that had set him on his quest: I lift my eyes up unto the mountains, where does my help come from? Here he was, in the mountains. But the verse said his help came from the Lord. Not the rocks, not the trees, not even the sun and the magnificent bowl of blue above. It was peaceful here, but the peace wasn't because of the place.

Will pulled the Bible out of the oilskin pouch and began to read. In First Kings, he read the story of Elijah and the storm—God was not in the wind. Even before that, when Elijah was feeling sorry for himself and ran away to the mountain of Horeb, for what was he searching? God asked Elijah why he was there, just like the wolf in

Will's dream. How many times had people on this journey asked him why he was there? Was he feeling sorry for himself because of the war, the deaths, losing Jenny, losing everything he knew? He'd been searching for peace—but maybe the wrong kind. Everywhere there were men, and there was trouble, fighting, and jealousy. Perhaps no place or person had the peace he was seeking.

He flipped through his Bible some more. He stood and walked onto the outcropping that was the tip of Wolverine Peak. There were sheer drops on both sides, but from here, he could see everything— the whole world, it seemed. He sat and read some more. His eye caught the mention of Elijah in the New Testament that he prayed, and for three years it didn't rain, and Elijah was a man like him. If Elijah could do that, what would God do for him if he prayed? Will remembered that Jesus promised he would give peace, peace beyond understanding, not like the peace of the world.

"Lord, I think I've been running from you, searching, but not for your peace, and not looking in the right places. Heal me, Lord, give me your peace. Forgive me, Lord, and teach me how to give peace to others."

Will prayed in silence for a while, then said, "Lord grant me success. I need to find that eagle."

He stuffed everything back in the oilskin and bent over to pick up his belongings. He walked along the ridge, searching the sky for the eagle's return. He bent forward listening, but the wind whipped away any possibility of hearing the eagle or Lightning below—if he was still there.

As he straightened, an arrow nicked his wrist. He whirled in time to see Kajika near the aerie, fitting another arrow onto the bow. There was nowhere to run or hide. Will bent down, charging head first, just like he'd done in the schoolyard as a boy, running as fast as he could toward Kajika and drawing Dove's knife.

Any second, he expected to feel the searing burn of an arrow in a leg or his gut, but nothing came. He slashed with the knife in front of him, cutting the bowstring, and then his head rammed into Kajika's midsection, knocking him backward. They rolled on the ground, Kajika grabbing Will's knife arm at the wrist, seeking to knock it loose.

Will felt desperate. Kajika was bulkier and more muscular. He pushed with a leg, and they rolled again. This time, instead of trying to push the knife into Kajika, he made a quick thrust, broke away, and pulled the knife hand against Kajika's thumb. Retreat was the better strategy

He broke free and ran a short way down the plateau. He was breathing hard; his heart thundered against his ribs. He turned to face Kajika, his back to the canyon, breathing a prayer for help.

Kajika shook himself, rising to his feet, and pulled a knife.

He sneered, "Weak little white man! You are like a woman. Will you beg for your life, or die like a man? I will carve out your heart and feed you to the birds!"

He assumed a crouch, like an experienced knife fighter, and approached Will.

Will knew he could not overpower him. Kajika slashed at him, and he jumped aside, slashing back at the extended arm. Kajika feinted a stab to his right, then cut left, catching Will's arm just above the elbow. Will felt burning and the stickiness of blood, but he couldn't even look at the wound, concentrating on his opponent. Kajika moved in closer. Will quickly slashed crossways at the neck level, then down the chest, catching him above the belly and downward, drawing blood. Kajika jumped back in surprise but then came forward again more warily. Will didn't wait—he slashed in an X pattern, first one way, then another, forcing Kajika to retreat.

The loss of blood made Will feel faint. If he lost consciousness, he knew he'd be dead. Kajika yelled a war cry and charged, seeking to overpower him, slashing left and right as he came. Will parried the thrust, then jumped aside. Kajika realized he'd gone too fast. He shouted, but it was too late—without Will in the way, he went hurtling out over the cliff edge, falling, his scream ringing out across the mountains.

He was gone. Will staggered away from the cliff edge, sprawling into blackness.

When Will became conscious, he had no idea how long he'd lain there. His head throbbed, but the bleeding had stopped. He lay still for a few minutes, dragged himself to all fours, and then stood, breathing hard in the thin air from the effort.

He walked over to his shelter and drank some water. Wrapping himself in the bedroll, Will ate some venison, resting to gather strength for the downward journey. He prayed, asking forgiveness for himself and Kajika. He knew what he had to do. He gathered his belongings and inched his way down to where he'd left Lightning. He needed to get back to Dusty and get help for Kajika—if he still lived.

CHAPTER FIFTEEN

Will stumbled into the village. He was walking in a nightmare. Lightning trotted along behind, whining. It was strangely quiet. People weren't out. He went to Lone Bear's lodge. The flaps were shut. He wanted to scream for help, but he knew it would only dishonor him and do no good. He went around to Washakie's tent, and the old man motioned him to enter.

"Where is everyone?"

"You are hurt. Rest and smoke." He motioned to his wife to get water and call the healer.

"We have to go back! Kajika is hurt, maybe dead. I need to get help for him. I have to tell you . . . Kajika attacked me. I'd just found the eagle. God spoke to me, and I knew what to do. I had to defend myself." Will stopped, the memory hitting him hard, his face twisting in pain. "He charged me with a knife. I dodged, and he fell a long way into the canyon. I think he's dead, but we need to go find him. I'll need help to get him back."

Washakie was silent, impassive. After a long while, he spoke. "I too have news. Since you left, my niece Dove and her family have become very sick. Everyone in the village keeps to themselves so that the sickness does not spread. I have heard from my brothers at the lake that the sickness is there also."

Will swung around, startled. "Dove is sick? I should go to her."

"I would counsel patience. Her family is not well. When they hear of Kajika's fall, they may not welcome you. There will be great sadness. You should rest and gain strength. Kajika's family will want you to show them where he fell, so that they may help his spirit on its journey."

"But I have some healing skill. I could help her."

Washakie held his gaze. "I believe your heart is true, as Gabe told me. Not all will see it that way. If you act as a shaman, a healer toward her without being asked, and she dies, they will hold you responsible for her life. If she dies, they might kill you, and I could not stop them. If they ask you, then you must try, or they may wish to kill you also. It is our way."

Washakie's wife came and bid Will to lay on a robe. She bathed and bandaged the wound and poured whiskey on it, which caused Will's face to be ashen, and he clenched his teeth to avoid crying out. He knew that to show pain was a disgrace, and he did not want to lose Washakie's respect.

Washakie bent over him.

"Sleep now. When you wake, we will have food and speak more."

Dove lay on robes in her parents' tipi. She felt hot, sweaty, and every brush of her buckskin dress on her skin burned and itched. When she looked at her hand, red spots were everywhere. She let her arm sink back down. She moaned and called for her mother, but no one came. Her mother, sister, and father all lay on robes nearby. Her brother had gone to another lodge since he was not sick. She was always thirsty, but there was no one to bring water. Getting up to relieve herself was torture. Darkness, darkness all around. Where was Will? Did he have a vision? Did something happen to him? Would the evil little people come and carry her to the land of shadows?

Her head hurt, and she ached all over. She'd never felt so ill. Was this what it was like to die?

She passed out; she didn't know for how long. When she came back, her stomach rumbled with hunger. She heard a noise, a loud keening cry. Had someone died of the sickness? The wails increased. Water. She had to have water. With supreme effort, she used her elbows to push up and rise to a half-sitting position. Dove looked around and saw Laughing Moon lying on her furs next to her mother. Neither seemed awake. Her father groaned and moved listlessly, delirious in fever. Lone Bear began to wave his arms, as though fighting an enemy.

Sick or not, she had to do something. She pushed herself with a grimace to a full sitting position, grabbed one of the tipi's supports to pull herself up, and stood, tottering as though she might fall.

She took two steps, staggered, and then two steps more, from the back of the tipi to the door. The fire in the center had almost gone out, just a few coals left, making whisps of smoke rising to the top and through the hole. She pulled out the pieces of bone that held the flaps closed and threw it open. Her eyes hurt at the brightness of the day, and suddenly she felt chilled to the bone. She wanted to turn, to lie back down, burrow into the buffalo robes. But there had to be water. Glancing around, she saw a waterskin. How would she ever make it to the river and back?

Dove picked it up and started for the river, but she fell, tripping over a tree root she hadn't seen.

Maybe she should stay still. Maybe her spirit would find its way to the good lands. What was it Will told her? Jesus? That was it . . . Limping Wolf told her Jesus loved her, made Will like he was. Maybe this Jesus would come and guide her there.

She felt gentle hands on her shoulders, reaching under her, lifting her. She looked up and saw her cousin, Fat Elk Woman, on one side and Will on the other, raising her, carrying her back to the tipi.

After they had her on the robes again, Will came with the waterskin, full of cold, refreshing water.

"Drink slow now. Not too much at once."

"Cold. So cold."

"Yeah, the water is snowmelt."

"I'm cold. Freezing. Don't leave me."

"I'm here. We need to get you some food. You're burning up with fever."

"First hot, then cold."

He covered her with the robe.

The tipi flap opened, and the shaman entered.

"Washakie says Lone Bear is not able to ask me to help, so he asks, both for you and Dove."

"Take care of her. Don't worry about me."

"Washakie will pay for you both." He handed Will some bread spread with a thick green paste. "Eat this, and drink some whiskey."

He turned to Fat Elk Woman, standing in the doorway. "Make her a broth, not too thick, from venison or elk." She hurried to obey.

"Dove? Dove!"

When she didn't respond, he panicked. He felt her wrist. Her heart was still beating, and her breasts rose and fell. She was alive, then, but not conscious. Perhaps resting was best. He prayed silently. He didn't know what the sickness was. He'd seen enough smallpox in Camp Douglas to realize it wasn't that. The large angry red spots all over her face, neck, and shoulders—everywhere visible— indicated it was some type of virulent infectious rash.

He sat and watched her. She began sweating again and started thrashing. He took the buffalo robe off her. He wet a cloth with the water from the skin, putting it on her forehead.

Will heard more crying and keening outside—Kajika's family. How long before they would insist he leave to find the body? And what would they do? Would they blame him and try to kill him there? He pushed the thought aside. All that mattered now was Dove. He'd deal with everything else later.

Her eyes fluttered open. She tried a weak smile, seeing Will leaning over her. Fat Elk Woman returned carrying a pottery bowl of steaming broth and a wooden spoon. Will propped Dove's head up and supported her shoulders with his leg, spooning the broth into her as she could manage it.

Limping Wolf came in, took in the scene, and began helping with water for the rest of the family. When Will saw him motion, he let Dove rest, laying her back down, and followed the preacher out of the lodge.

"It's measles; you know that, don't you?"

"No, I . . ."

"There's nothing we can do but make them comfortable. There's no cure. There are no herbs or magic potions. We can pray, but the outcome is up to God."

"But Dove . . . she's young; she's strong. And Lone Bear, he's a tough old man. They have to pull through."

"Son, you know better. You say you were in prison during the war. How many good men died—young men, who were in good shape? And for all sorts of reasons. If it helps, Dove did talk to me while you were gone. She said she doesn't understand all the markings in that book of yours, but she wanted to trust this Jesus if it meant being closer to the Great Mystery and you. That was just before she got sick. Now go on back to her. She needs you. If anything can pull her through, it will be your love and care—and God's mercy."

Will walked back into the tent. He noticed the glowering stares of Kajika's father and brother. It seemed likely there would be trouble.

All that night, Dove passed in and out of consciousness. Will tried to feed her, but by the middle of the next day, she wouldn't eat. She barely responded to drops of water on her tongue. She no longer thrashed and wasn't talking. The fever seemed to grow rather than break.

Will sat with her all night. Sleep was the last thing he wanted, even if he had to shake himself a few times to keep from dropping off. He stroked her face, kept the cloth damp and gave her drops of water when she would take them.

When dawn's rays found their way into the tent, he could see her chest barely moved. The pulse in her arm was weak and erratic. Finally, it stopped altogether. Dove was gone.

Will held the red spotted lifeless hand as it grew colder. He was no stranger to death, even the death of friends—but this was different. Dove was his love, his life. How could God take her, just when she agreed to be with Him?

After sitting for perhaps an hour, the sobs came. Will didn't care who saw or heard. He felt a pain in his chest like he could hardly breathe. His brain refused to function.

Finally, he rose, walked out of the tent, and went to Washakie. "She's gone," he said. "There's nothing left to fight for."

CHAPTER SIXTEEN

Will helped to build the funeral stand. Lone Bear was back on his feet, but the sorrow of losing his daughter and the effects of the stress made him seem like a ghost. Laughing Moon was so sad, she barely even looked up as she went about her chores. Her mother was sick with grief, staring into space. Fat Elk Woman and Laughing Moon prepared Dove's body, dressing her in her finery and making sure she had a bow, her knife, her fire drill, and other necessities for the after world. Will said nothing as they did this, figuring leaving them alone in the customs would help their grief. He controlled himself with difficulty as he and Lone Bear lifted her, one last time, to the funeral platform, where she could always see the stars and roam among them.

Washakie came over to Will.

"What will you do now?"

"I do not know. With Dove, I was beginning to find peace from the war. God has shown me that my peace lies in Him, not a place or a person. But my heart is torn in two at her death."

"You cannot stay here," said Washakie.

"I know. I had hoped to ask Dove to follow me to another place with my people. I think Lone Bear would have allowed it."

"Perhaps. But the Great Mystery did not. Yet he gave you a gift, the light of her life, her love for a time. That is worth a great deal."

"Yes, it is. We have a saying among my people—perhaps you know it. 'The Lord gives, and the Lord takes away. Blessed be the name of the Lord.'"

"I hope your heart mends and you keep your peace. I suggest you go south and west from here. You will come to the white man's road through the mountains. Follow it to the post that used to be owned by my friend Old Gabe. You will be able to trade the horses you won for supplies. You will be safe there until you decide what to do. Kajika is in fever. But it may be that in a few days or weeks, he will think of you again and desire revenge. You must go before that happens. You have a good horse and four others besides. I will give you some food. You have your revolver and your rifles. I make you a gift of this pipe and this knife. Other Shoshone will recognize the pipe. Show them, and you will be safe with them unless you find Pocatello, who hates all whites."

"You are kind and generous. If there is anything I can ever do for you, don't be slow to ask."

"It may be that our paths will cross again. But if not, stay safe. Our camp will move soon. We will not remain where someone has died."

The next morning, with Laughing Moon and Fat Elk Woman helping, Will packed his things and strung his horses together in a line behind Dusty. Lightning leaned his head against Will and thumped his tail. The sun rose above the trees. Will mounted, waved, and rode out of the village, following Washakie's advice about Fort Bridger.

His mind was in a fog of grief, but he knew that God had a plan for him, though he did not see it. He had to move forward and see where the trail led.

Author's Notes

The events detailed here for Will Crump are entirely my invention. During the period of this narrative, no one knows where the historical Will Crump was or what he was doing. There are a few indicators that he went west to the mountains after the Civil War, but no firm documentation.

Wolverine and Gannett Peak were not named officially until the early twentieth century. The names are used in the text as a point of reference for the reader.

Crazy Woman Creek was the name assigned by traders in the middle 1800s. There are many legends about the "Crazy Woman." One says it was named for an Indian woman, left to live alone in her tipi there, who went insane. The more common story told is the violent and tragic tale of the settler who witnessed the capture and scalping of her husband by Indians, which drove her to insanity, similar to that chronicled in the Hollywood movie, Jeremiah Johnson. The Shoshone name for the location during that period is unknown.

The character of Dove is entirely fictional. Many Shoshone had involvement with the Latter-Day Saints. Cheyenne, Lakota (Sioux), Crow, Pawnee, and Arapahoe were all traditional enemies of the Shoshone; in some cases, relations are still not cordial. Tribal alliances shifted over the years, but in the period of the story, Lakota and Brule were on the rise.

The historical characters of the book, such as Patrick Conner, Washakie, Fetterman, Grummond, Carrington, and Jim Bridger, have been portrayed in action and dialogue as close to history as I could make them. Any errors are mine or due to lack of information. Mrs. Francis Carrington's account, My Army Life, has served as the source for some of this information.

Fort Laramie on the High Plains by Douglas McChristian and Fort Laramie National Historic Site were the sources of material on the fort during the period of this story. There were often Crow and Sioux in and around the fort. There was a group of Sioux that stayed near the fort at various times called the "Laramie Loafers." At other times, especially those of tension with the whites, there were no Native Americans around the fort. During this period, the fort had no walls. At other times, there were adobe walls around it. Restrictions on Native Americans on the fort premises are my invention.

I am indebted to Christopher Loether and Drusilla Gould of Idaho State University (ISU), and Darren Parry, Chairman of the Western Shoshone, for their patient answering of questions regarding Shoshone customs and life. The Smithsonian Handbook of North American Indian Life also provided cultural information. My friend Kay Flowers of the ISU library pointed me to Chris and Drusilla. Any errors in Shoshone thought or custom are my own.

I obtained further insight into Shoshone and Plains Native American life from Elijah Nicholas Wilson's first-person account of his life with Washakie and the Shoshone.

The University of Utah's Shoshone language project provided the Shoshone words in the text of the book; any mistakes in their usage are mine.

Stanley Vestal's excellent book Jim Bridger, Mountain Man provided insight into the character, habits, and whereabouts of Bridger and an account of the Tongue River battle.

Darren Parry's Bear River Massacre book and his tour of the massacre site with me are the sources of information on Bear River, along with the account and maps of Sergeant Beach, a soldier who was there.

http://www.legendsofamerica.com/na-proverbs provided the quote about thunder in the mouth and lightning in the hand, and is Apache in origin.

Ella Clark's Indian Legends of the Northern Rockies provided the Shoshone creation story and their flood narrative, verified through Darren Parry, as well as other aspects of Shoshone spiritual life.

Walter Martin's Kingdom of the Cults and official web pages

of the Church of the Latter-Day Saints provided the information for Mormon beliefs and doctrines.

The United States government carried out a wilful program of genocide on many Native American tribes. Countless Native Americans died of diseases brought to them by European immigrants, for which they had no natural resistance. Estimates range as high as eighteen million Native Americans in North America before the European invasions. Death tolls from diseases reached as high as eighty percent.

The government failed to understand that there was no central governing authority among the Native Americans. The concept of a chief or central leader was mostly fiction. An individual might lead a war party or a buffalo hunt, but family bands combined and split with the seasons, and even within these, each man was free to go his own way. The nomadic hunter-gatherer lifestyle, dependent on game, precluded large permanent groups of Native Americans. Thus signatories of treaties on the Native American side represented a small fraction of their tribes rather than the agreement of the tribe as a whole. Red Cloud managed an alliance of tribes of short duration, resulting in forcing the treaty of 1868 on Native American terms. Both Red Cloud and Spotted Tail gave up war after touring the East at President Grant's invitation and seeing that there was no possibility of ultimate Native American military victory.

The Native American tribes warred upon each other and had traditional enemies long before the arrival of Europeans. While white man's concept of land ownership was unknown among them, there were broad territorial claims, and the Native Americans took territory from one another. During the period of the book, the Sioux in particular were expanding into lands they had not previously held. The notion that the white men came and stole land is not entirely accurate in that respect—rather, men of varying races and tribes took land from one another, as has happened everywhere down through history.

Let us hope we can put our differences aside and reach out to one another—Across the Great Divide.

Across the Great Divide

214

Michael L. Ross

Additional Diagrams

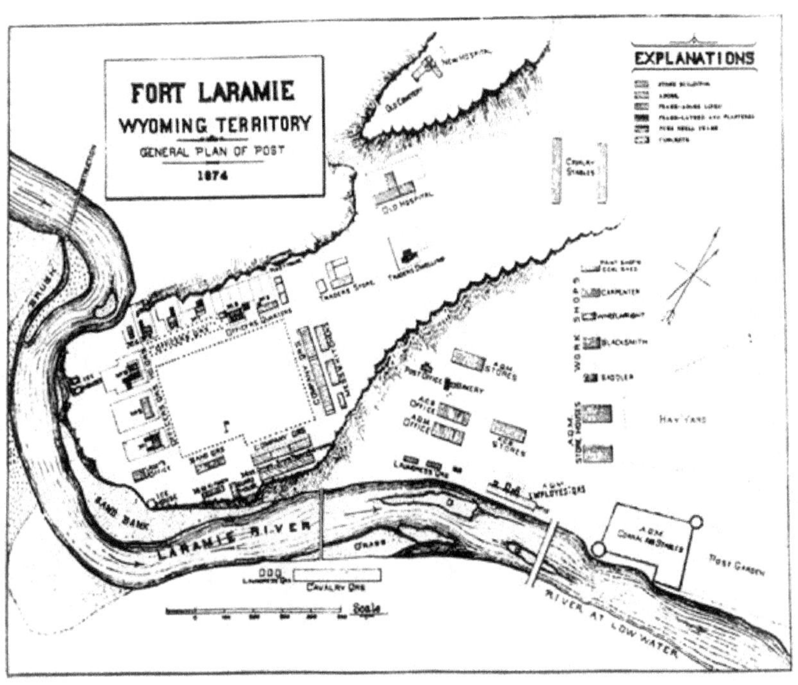

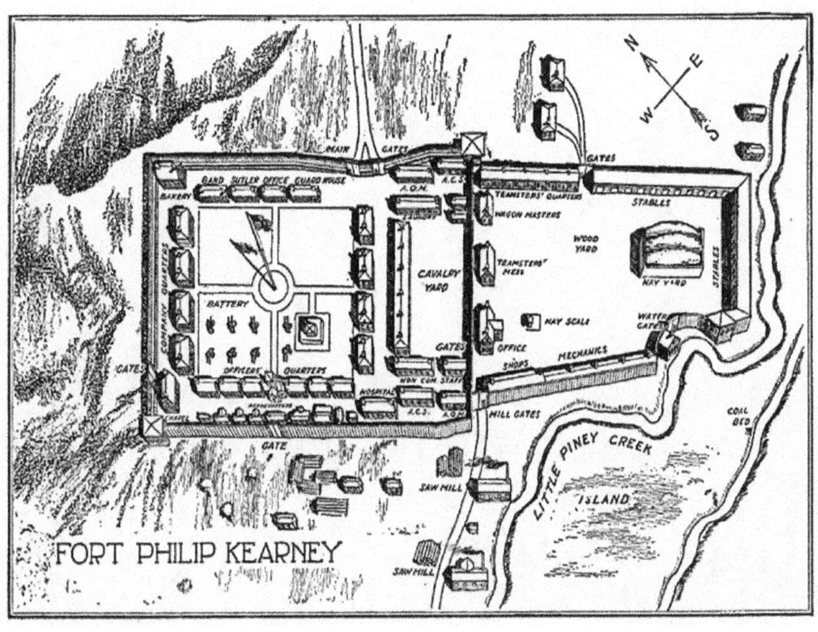
MAIN GATES
A.Q.M.
A.C.S.
BAND SUTLER OFFICE GUARD HOUSE
BAKERY
COMPANY QUARTERS
BATTERY
OFFICERS QUARTERS
HEADQUARTERS
GATES
HAZEL
GATE
HOSPITAL
NON COM STAFF
A.C.S. A.Q.M.
CAVALRY YARD
GATES
TEAMSTERS' QUARTERS
WAGON MASTERS
TEAMSTERS' MESS
OFFICE
SHOPS MECHANICS
HAY SCALE
WOOD YARD
STABLES
HAY YARD
STABLES
GATES
WATER GATE
MILL GATES
SAW MILL
SAW MILL
LITTLE PINEY CREEK
ISLAND
COAL BED
FORT PHILIP KEARNEY
N
E
W
S